SUNNY VIEW PARK

I0556514

Thomas P. Baier

HATCHBACK Publishing
Genesee, Michigan

Sunny View Park
©2014 Thomas P. Baier

HATCHBACK Publishing, LLC.
P.O. Box 494
Genesee, Michigan 48437
Since 2005
www.hatchbackpublishing.com

Illustration by Alicia Deloach

Library of Congress Control Number
2014954188
ISBN: 978-0-9906859-6-8
10 9 8 7 6 5 4 3 2 1
First Edition
Printed in the United States of America

For Worldwide Distribution

Dedication

To Bailey

Sunny View Park

Dedication
Table of Contents

"It is the supreme art of the teacher to awaken joy
in creative expression and knowledge."
Albert Einstein

"A person who won't read has no advantage over one who can't read."
Mark Twain

"You cannot open a book without learning something."
Confucius

ASSIGNMENT

Cassiopeia, forever relegated to the northern hemisphere, once again found herself gazing on the miniature sphere designated as Earth. As she focused her sights, her starry eyes telescoped upon the characteristic brown and green mitten-shaped mass. Through eons, it has been geographically surrounded by five beautiful blue bodies of water. Investigating closer, she narrowed her study upon a northeastern sector of that state which hid the tiny hamlet of a town called Lincoln. It is in this very village the assignment begins.

Paul's eyes achingly popped wide open. Alone in his dark bedroom, the stabbing fear of the unknown startled him from his wayward dreams. Lying on his back with his small body frame melted into the bed, he gazed at the ceiling. Silence echoed the blackness like a starless universe. As he lay there frozen, unanswered questions were trapping him in a world of doubt and indecision. Procrastination, once again, was holding him captive.

Paul always convinced himself that he did his best under pressure. Many times he would cram information into a coffee-filled cranium the night before an important exam. Sometimes he would inventively create a gift for a friend or relative, only to find himself rushing around the last minute to complete the project. He would even try to see if he could squeeze one more mile out of a steadily evaporating tank of gasoline before he would have to relent and invest another dollar for more fuel. He would go to the extent to tell himself that he would eventually bestow thanks to his Creator for successfully rescuing him out of a devilishly twisted predicament. Well, once again a deadline was looming and there seemed to be no alternative. The pressure was becoming insurmountable. As he had done so many times before, he was privately turning to Him for help.

This time his adversary was Mr. Ian Sain. He was the Principal and the school's Senior Yearbook Advisor. He was also 'The Lincoln Lecturer' school Newspaper Editor, High School Drama Coach and the 'Young Politicians' Debate Counselor. Basically, if it had anything to do with the written word, Mr. Sain was involved. In fact, he had earned the moniker 'Sir Britannica' by a small group of the not so academically inclined. He was though, one of the nicest people on the small faculty staff at Lincoln High. Much to Paul's chagrin, Mr. Sain had discreetly declared war by announcing that Paul was his appointee to deliver a speech at the year's end graduation ceremonies.

Paul knew he was well qualified to address his fellow classmates with a simple oration. In fact, he had reached his goal of achieving high honors in his rigorously challenged college preparatory program of studies. In this small Class D designated school, he knew everyone in the senior class. So, the formalities of the speech itself or publicly speaking in the presence of his peers was not the problem. It was the precision of impact with which Paul wanted to drive home a message to his fellow classmates that concerned him. It was this same type of self-imposed stress that Paul, somewhat of a perfectionist, so routinely subjected himself to with many seemingly mundane daily activities. Still, he wondered, why did he have to be the chosen one? Why not another student or one of the class officers?

The more he thought about it the more he fidgeted under his covers. Restlessness and apprehension evolved into anxiety and frustration. Cold sweats turned into goose bumped tremors while the alarm clock on his side table methodically marched through the digital minutes of the night. Surrendering, Paul scrunched the blankets in his fists and pulled the covers to his chin as he coiled into the fetal position. As he struggled to fall back asleep, Paul's thoughts raced as he became a victim to his own mind. Justifying an answer, Paul finally realized what he was putting himself through, conceded and muttered to himself . . . "the adversary is me."

ATTITUDE

The weekend had arrived. Paul smiled to himself because he always welcomed a slight reprieve from his studies. The euphoria, however, was quickly replaced to agitation as the thoughts of preparing the graduation speech obtrusively invaded his harmonic mood. It was early March, so he had about ten weeks before he would need to have his assignment completed. Even though he had ample time, he still was not having any creative ideas of what his topic might be. He worried if he could not think of anything notable, Memorial Day was going to have an entirely different meaning for him.

Paul glanced out the window. The slight swaying of weeping willow branches were witness to the fanning breeze. Looking at the wet sidewalk, he concluded the long, hard grasp winter had on Mother Earth was releasing its grip as the final traces of snow were melting. Even though the lengthy cold season had sapped some of Paul's strength, his attitude was formidable. As his thoughts wandered, he couldn't help but remember a quote he had read which was made famous by automotive pioneer Henry Ford: "Whether you think you can, or you think you can't - you're right." Reflecting on this, Paul reenergized as he vowed to make progress on his task. He had been an isolated prisoner of winter long enough and wanted to take action because Father Time never waits or stands still. Paul decided to venture where he always received inspiration. He had to visit Sunny View Park.

Sunny View Park was Paul's sanctuary. The serenity and security it provided was a remedial retreat from the advancing uncertainty of his adolescence. Although his visitations were in solitude, Paul always felt that he was among friends. Though a reassuring calmness wrapped its arms around him, Paul felt a giddiness deep down in his soul like a child opening presents on Christmas morning.

Shuffling along, Paul absorbed the sights and sounds of wildlife and nature. A woodpecker diligently rat-a-tat-tapped for insects burrowed into the bark of a tree. Sparrows fleeted from tree branches to tree limbs, landing unsteadily and incessantly flapping their wings while trying to regain their balance. Squirrels played tag, stopping from time to time and scolding Paul for intruding on their territory and disrupting their fun. A chipmunk zipped across a hedge, bounding outstretched like a scene from Superman. The air was fresh, crisp and clean. The newly budding trees towered over Paul like giant strategically placed fingers resembling a skeletal canopy. Beneath his feet, sopping wet dead leaves from the autumn past were cushioning his every step as he marveled at the vibrant blue sky. Paul was in his panorama of perfection.

As he strolled along, Paul came upon the statue whom he had nicknamed 'The Professor.' Paul guessed from the base of the graying concrete pedestal it must have risen twelve feet tall. It commanded an impressive presence and though no reference on the stone offered a clue, it had an uncanny stoic resemblance to George Washington, as depicted in the painting of him crossing the Delaware. Paul would always pause and reflect as he became mesmerized by its dominance. Usually, he could not help but think of the famous artist Michelangelo when he sculpted the great David out of stone.

Every time Paul studied 'The Professor' he seemed to observe something different. His long majestic overcoat, unbuttoned, rested squarely on his broad shoulders as it tapered down to his knees. His legs, slightly bent, supported his upper torso as his back shifted slightly to the left. His right arm, comfortably resting against his side, had a slight crook at the elbow. His left arm, at a much sharper angle, was so positioned that his forearm was upright and the palm of his hand was facing him. He was holding a small book and seemed to be addressing an audience with important information. It was at this point that Paul became totally occupied with the statue and began to notice something different. As he peered toward the eyes, he could see intent. 'The Professor' appeared as though he was trying to explain an observation, teaching a lesson or offering instruction in a matter of relevance which was obviously simple to him but hard for others to understand. Paul, engrossed in thought, tried to imagine what he might be lecturing about when suddenly a voice out of nowhere surprisingly alarmed him.

"Hello, there, young man." Paul had not even noticed behind him an old man was sitting on one of two park benches that faced the front of the statue. Nestled between the benches lay a collie, curled in a semi-circle with his head resting on its paws. Paul assumed the old man had stopped to rest while taking his dog out for a walk.

"Hi," Paul curtly replied. Being caught off guard, his response was more of a defense mechanism than a cordial salutation.

"Beautiful morning, is it not?" the old man added as he gave a tight lipped smile and nodded his head. He was trying to establish harmony in this somewhat awkward introduction.

"Uh, yeah, pretty nice," Paul agreed. He was surveying the situation as well as trying to keep his composure. Paul became a little irritated if he was interrupted when he was fully occupied.

"He is grand, is he not?" the old man continued as he sized up 'The Professor' from head to foot.

"Yeah, if you say so," Paul shrugged. In fact, Paul was quite impressed with 'The Professor' yet tried to contain his appreciation. He was in no humor to become engaged in a conversation with an old fogy who was entertaining senility.

With his right hand cupping the top of an old wooden staff for balance, the old man then reached down with his left hand and patted the dog on its head. Then, as he looked up and his smile grew into a grin, he leaned forward with slow and deliberate words, "We have been watching you. What have you been pondering as you were admiring this magnificently sculpted massive piece of rock?"

Paul had actually completely forgotten what he was thinking. Trying to stifle the conversation, he abruptly retorted, "Nothing!"

"Oh, ho," the old man countered. "One cannot set his eyes upon something as marvelous as this and not have a single thought come to mind." The old man continued to stare at Paul. He was not going to allow this conversation to dissolve into a trite exchange of meaningless ideas.

Paul relented, "I guess I was just wondering what he was reading," as he looked up to 'The Professor' and zeroed in on the book.

"And, what do you think he is reading?" the old man asked as he tried to pick up the tempo of the dialogue.

Paul answered succinctly, "I don't know! Whatever!" still bothered by his intruder.

Sighing heavily, the old man looked back down to the dog and exhaustingly compromised, "Well, maybe we can figure it out."

At this point, Paul tried to earnestly decipher who this old man was, what he was doing and why he was doing it. While Paul had reservations about the authenticity of this old soul, he could not help but see the resemblances between him and two other great men of history in their elder years. The first person Paul thought of when he saw the old man was Albert Einstein. In their own way, both were quite unassuming, modest and displaying an element of tenderness. Though somewhat unkempt, they also commanded respect and attention from their age earned experience. By knowing them, one was honored with a great privilege. The other was Mark Twain. Paul could sense the old man had a folksy wisdom about him and a wry sense of humor. Also, it was evident that a persnickety persistence pervaded his actions. All seemed to have the same build, including the chiseled look of a weathered seaman and the self-assuredness of their individual missions seemed to coalescence their personalities.

The old man then slowly rose from the bench and steadied himself, wrapping both hands around the top of his cane. He, too, had an old overcoat, unbuttoned and draping to his knees. Carefully, he stepped toward Paul. At this cue, the dog also struggled to lift itself from its contented spot, forelegs first and then its hind quarters. Together, they lumbered toward Paul like the last duo of a regiment fatigued by war.

"It doesn't matter . . . it's not that important," Paul exasperated. He could not understand where the conversation was heading and was becoming increasingly irritated with the uninvited visitor.

Slowly, the old man crept closer to Paul and reaching out, wrapped his right hand around Paul's forearm. Then, he sternly peered into Paul's eyes and carefully replied, "Yes, it is that important." He hesitated, calculatingly paused and finished, "Plus . . . it does matter."

"What's important? What matters?" Paul shot back. He was becoming greatly incensed that this hobo was about to lecture him on something he did not even know what they were talking about. He shook the old man's grasp from his arm and backed away from him.

"Let me borrow a word from your infinite repertoire of vocabulary words," the old man's voice, in almost a scolding vein, suddenly became more harsh and direct. "Whatever. Whatever is, in life, is important. And, whatever is important . . . matters. Our world contains a plethora of information. By a grand design, everything works and obeys laws in conjunction with each other. From the tiniest of microscopic molecules to the extended edges of the universe and everything contained therein, life matters. It harbors its secrets until the time is ripe to reveal its influence. Now, whether it is important to you is not a question to be debated. The point is, life is important and it matters."

Paul's mind was swimming from the old man's philosophic answer. "Man, you don't have to get an attitude. Cool it. Relax!" Paul's weakness, impatience, was revealing itself. That, along with sarcasm, was one of the other darker areas of his personality that he was trying to improve upon.

"You are quite correct, young man, I do not have to get an attitude. Nor do you. However, since we are on the subject of, shall I say, mind management, there is one more thing that I would like to add to your use of the word 'whatever.' Whatever . . . ," but just as he was about to finish his reply a squirrel darted across a berm about twenty feet away.

The old collie, taken by surprise, perked up his ears and set his sights on the rodent. He stood up, tail straightened and in frozen concentration analyzed the situation. In a frenzy, he darted toward the squirrel, gurgling growls as a warning that it had invaded his domain. The chase ensued. Then, almost in unison, as the squirrel found refuge in a nearby tree, the old collie stopped cold in his tracks. The dog did not even attempt to trail the squirrel to the base of the tree. It was in fact, hard to determine whether the squirrel had made a safe getaway or that the old dog turned sympathetic and let it go. Whatever the case, the collie seemed obliged to remain within his boundaries as the squirrel now safely perched on a tree limb, sat comically scolding his predator.

"What's up with your dog?" Paul was grinning ear to ear as he just witnessed a spastic fuzz ball outwit a seasoned hunter. "He seemed pretty intent on having a new play toy when all of a sudden he just gave up. Where's his determination?"

The rubbery faced grin returned to the old man's face as he sat down. "First of all, he is not my dog. But, at times when I come to this park, my old friend finds his way to me and provides unconditional comfort. He has a sense of pure loyalty. He has a family. I just kind of adopt him for a very small portion of the day whenever I come here. Our time together is quite special." The old man paused as in reflection of an idea and continued. "Anyway, returning to your remarks about the dog's behavior concerning his intent and resoluteness. Well, what you just attested to happens fairly regularly. Every so often, while we are enjoying each other's company, a squirrel like the one you just saw, a chipmunk or even a brave cat will wander within his view. And, like he just did, he will give chase to the harried creature. He zips out of here like a bullet. But, like now, he will always stop short of his prize. The best I can figure is . . . have you ever heard of an unseen fence?"

Paul had but now he was preoccupied with the old man's storytelling and did not want to interrupt. He only raised his eyebrows encouraging the old man to continue.

"It is something like a barb wired fence, but you do not see it." As he explained this concept, he brought his hands up in front of his chest as if he was holding a ball, and shook them for emphasis. "Animals, usually dogs, are trained to stay within a safe area decided by their trainers. If they venture beyond their boundaries, they will be slightly, not inhumanely, shocked and this deters them from exploring further. Through repetition and proper reinforcement, the animal learns to remain within a controlled setting. I have deduced that this is the situation with our friend, here. We are witnessing the efforts of someone who has trained his pet to stay within a predetermined area of this park. For whatever reason, he has allowed him to occupy a certain area in a conscientiously protective manner. I have seen it many times in homeowner's yards. I would not even be surprised if its master is watching us now from one of those nearby houses."

Paul peered at the old man and tried to summarize what he had just heard. "You mean that he's afraid to go further than he thinks he can? He has been conditioned to believe that he cannot go one step further and that he has doubts about his capabilities?"

"Basically," the old man resounded, confirming Paul's thoughts.

Paul, now completely absorbed in the conversation, quickly added, "I've heard of something like that before. Except, I heard they do this with circus elephants. The trainer secures a chain around the ankle of a baby elephant. And, as it tries to roam, the elephant is held within a confined space as the links of the chain tighten. It is being conditioned at a very young age. Then, after the chains are removed, the elephant believes in its confinement, and has lost its will to venture into unknown territory."

"Exactly," the old man added. "And, unfortunately, four legged beasts are not the only creatures that share this condescending trait. This is the same principle that we, as humans, adopt when we strive to stretch ourselves beyond our safe zone. Our fear of the unknown keeps us in check. We never know what is on the other side of the invisible barrier if we do not spread our wings to soar above to greater heights."

The old man continued, "Let me explain. As youngsters, we are free, uninhibited, adventurous spirits. Untamed hellions, we are, conquering anything and everything that tries to stop us from what we are determined

16

to do with unabashed freedom. But, sadly, as we grow, we are protected from potential success from over protective parents, well intentioned friends, peer groups, and work associates. They try to save us from disappointment by "no", "do not try that", and "it will never work" theories. Sometimes, they will even say that they have tried something similar and that it did not work for them. They actually believe they are doing us a favor by saving us from ourselves. They forget to realize that a temporary setback is only a stepping stone toward a desired goal. A learning experience. As a result, by listening to these prophets of doom, we give up and do not try. A fear of failure is instilled in us, so we never realize our full potential. In essence, we deprive ourselves of opportunity because we now reflect on how negative events have happened to other people and we have lost our ambition. We give up before even trying and resign ourselves to being comfortable and secure."

"No pain, no gain," Paul added.

"Yes," the old man replied. "Safe, but in the long run, sorry." He paused, regained his thoughts and continued, "Now, where were we . . . ah, yes, this ties in perfectly. Whatever." Now, speaking once again more boldly he confidently spoke, "Whatever the mind of man can conceive and believe, it can achieve." Never, never forget that, young man. W. Clement Stone was a 'success through positive thinking' pioneer and coined that truism. With that belief, a person can go anywhere."

"That also has a lot to do with attitude, doesn't it?" Paul asked.

"Oh, yes," the old man agreed. At-ti-tude," slowly emphasizing each syllable with calculated deliberation. We do not have to 'get' an attitude, either, as you admonished me earlier. In fact," he smiled, "everybody already has one, anyway. It is what we have become by the way we look at life's events, how they impact us and how we react to them. Many times, we allow these external events to shape our personality. We surrender control of our emotions . . . good event equals good attitude, and conversely, bad event equals bad attitude. Actually, it should be the other way around. We should form our own positive attitude and let that be the way we perceive life. In the end, how we look at events - our choice - becomes habit and so goes our way of life. What many do not understand is that by donning a different pair of spectacles and viewing life differently, they will have a completely different perception of events. Viktor Frankl, a Nazi death camp survivor and internationally renowned psychiatrist, described it this way . . . 'Everything can be taken from a man but one thing: the last of the human freedoms - to choose one's attitude in any given set of circumstances, to choose one's own way.'"

"Do you think this is what 'The Professor' is reading about?" Paul inquired.

"Oh, of that I am not certain," the old man replied. "What I do believe, however, is that he is not reading, but rather teaching. Teaching."

By this time, the collie had returned and found his way back to the padded grassy area from which he so abruptly left. The old man also retreated to his place on the bench, rested his cane against its wooden slats and leaned back. With his palms resting on his knees, he carefully gazed up at the statue once again. He appeared to be relieved. It was the same look of self-satisfaction Mr. Sain would wear when he taught a lesson of life that the whole school understood. A small success.

Paul also steered his vision toward the statue. The seconds of silence seemed to stretch for hours. Finally, Paul decided to excuse himself. Lowering his eyes to the old man and with somewhat of a sheepish pronunciation he announced, "I guess I better get going."

"Yes," the old man nodded in contented agreement.

Paul slowly turned away and walked a few steps in his direction home. After a few paces more, a sudden feeling of isolation encased him. Shrugging it off, he continued homeward. The cold eeriness would not relent and he squiggled as he tried to shake the feeling. He wondered if the old man was analyzing his erratic movements. He looked back at the bench and saw the collie keeping an attentive vigil. The old man, however, was nowhere to be seen.

INTEGRITY

The week had flown by. Even though instructors were not assigning many homework projects, Paul was still struggling with his speech dilemma which was now only nine weeks away. Still he had no ideas and it kept gnawing at him like an advanced case of poison ivy. Every time he thought that he had it under control, it would crop up and needle him more.

The evenings were similar. Paul would hang out with his friends and watch television, play video games or surf the computer internet. But when he was ready to fall asleep for the night, the same questions would resurface in his mind. Why is Mr. Sain making me do this? Why couldn't he do something different? Why do they have to make such a big deal about graduation, anyway? Everyone will just forget about it when it's over.

Again, the weekend beckoned. Paul was not going to let something seemingly so far away interfere with what he wanted to do right now. He wanted instant gratification. He reasoned that he had earned the privilege to do as he pleased because he had been diligent about his routine duties during the week. Doing what he wanted now was his reward rather than planning for something that seemed like an eternity away. He thought he would just kick back and enjoy himself. Maybe something would happen and he wouldn't have to write the speech, or perhaps Mr. Sain would change his mind and have him do something that Paul wanted to do. If that happened, he wouldn't have to put as much effort into it. Yeah, that seemed like a good idea to Paul. Then he wouldn't have to try as hard. Once again, Paul felt better by rationalizing himself out of a task that he really knew he should have been prepared.

After breakfast, Paul was determined to go outside to enjoy the day before he would have to succumb to his chores. He wanted to resist the weekend regiment of his household responsibilities for as long as possible. Sometimes, he would motivate himself enough to jog to the street corner and back - a total distance of one-quarter mile. He would dream about being able to run further distances. Yes, he thought, this morning he would once again be resolute and decide to change his life. But, everything else would have to be just perfect before he would challenge himself. He eventually decided this just was not one of those times. He let external events dictate his choices. This routine would sometimes find himself questioning himself, his confidence and his abilities. He knew he was not being true to himself. Nevertheless, he dismissed these thoughts and replaced them with others.

Paul decided to go to Sunny View Park. As he headed to his retreat, his mind began to wander to last weekend's events when he met the old man. He could not figure out how the old curmudgeon had disappeared so quickly. Paul wondered where he lived, if he had a job and even if he had a family. He also wondered was he mad because Paul had been so sarcastic to him or would he even ever see him again.

The answer to Paul's last question came quicker than he thought. He had already entered the park and was casually approaching the statue. There he saw the old man shadowing the marvelous work of marble, peering at Paul as he came into view. His arms were outstretched forward, one hand atop of the other, palming the top of his cane. His tattered overcoat, unbuttoned, draped at his sides. His loose fitting baggy pants crumpled over the top of his well-traveled, dusty oxfords. With every step Paul could sense he was being studied. Their eyes focused and locked. Simultaneously, out of the corner of his eyes, Paul noticed the old man's comrade. On its haunches, the collie was at his side.

"Good morning, lad," the old man greeted.

"Hello," Paul politely replied, wondering what was to happen next.

"We have been waiting for you," the old man offered as he nodded his head toward the collie, yet keeping his gaze fixed on Paul.

Paul shrugged his shoulders and gave a slight tilt of his head, "Oh, yeah. Why's that?"

"More teaching. More lessons," the answers coming as a friendly but firm directive. "The capacity to learn is endless. And, we must test."

Flabbergasted, Paul could feel his eyelids forcefully and intermittently blinking rather than the smooth involuntarily movement of which people are normally unaware. Trying to clear his thinking, tunnel vision ensued and while his gaze remained centered on the faded gray eyes of the old man, his peripheral vision entertained the silhouette of the collie and the statue. Their presence reminded him of a browned, faded portrait reminiscent of the 1800's. Seemingly, he was captivated in time but in slow motion reality.

"Okay," Paul relented, as he lifted his right arm and deftly massaged his eyebrows with his fingers.

Seeing Paul becoming composed, the old man stepped back and repositioned his cane on the ground. A wiry smile broke across his chiseled cheeks as he rested his hands upon his staff once again. His eyes softened and in a slight raspy voice whispered, "Let us begin."

The old man paused for effect and stared down at the ground. He prodded his cane in the dirt, he lifted his head and asked, "What do you see below?"

Playing his little game, Paul glanced down and could barely decipher the outline of a raised, round object that was otherwise deeply embedded in the soil. The sparsely grown blades of weathered grass partially hid it from view but it was clear something was encrusted in the earth. Paul wondered how the old man ever noticed it. Nevertheless, as Paul knelt down and studied the object, he recognized the familiar details of the nation's sixteenth president. Yes, it was Abraham Lincoln gracing the face of a penny. It was also the namesake of Paul's school, Lincoln High. Someone had lost a penny and the old man had found it.

"Oh, boy, a whole penny!" Paul exclaimed, looking up at the old man with another of his sarcastic smirks.

"Yes, a penny," the old man hesitantly agreed.

"Do I pass? Did I learn something?" Paul was referring back to the original comment he was posed when the two of them met earlier.

"We shall see, my friend," the old man solemnly declared, "We shall see."

The old man gingerly squatted down and slowly reached for the coin. His arthritic fingers fumbled as he gently grasped the molded metal from its buried home. As he picked it up, the caked filth broke from its underside and fell to the ground like crumbs from a cookie. Inspecting the coin, he rose up and rocked the penny between his thumb and forefinger. Gently, as if not to mar the stamped portrait, he began to carefully smooth the dirt away. Rather than revealing a dull copper appearance, this one was different. It possessed a dull, lead toned appearance.

"Hey, why isn't it brown?" Paul asked as he leaned his head closer to the old man's hand.

The old man outstretched his thumb and forefinger as he displayed the coin more clearly. Then, as he raised his arm towards the sky replied,

"This, son, is a silver penny. It is made of zinc coated steel instead of copper alloy. It was minted during World War II when resources were scarce, at a premium and copper was needed for the war effort. Steel was cheaper. Their numbers are now few."

Becoming intrigued by this impromptu history lesson, Paul asked, "What's the date on it?"

"It appears to be 1943," he answered. "The year of my birth." A satisfying look developed across the old man's face as he, once again, methodically tottered the coin in his hand. "By the way," he added, "tell me your knowledge of the penny."

"Well, I know it doesn't buy as much as it used to," Paul said, trying to keep the conversation on the subject of history.

"A penny saved is a penny earned," the old man volunteered, as if beginning a game of trivia.

"Yeah, but I really don't understand that one. It doesn't make much . . . ha, ha . . . 'sense' to me." Paul thought he was clever interjecting the humor.

"It is a virtue - thrift," he explained without hesitation. Benjamin Franklin, shall I say, 'coined' the phrase as he was reinventing himself towards moral excellence."

"Hey, that was pretty good," Paul chuckled, referring to the old man's own play on words. "So, it seems that if you save up enough pennies, they'll add up and it will seem like you worked for them and got paid."

"Precisely," the old man concluded. "But, there is more to it than that. A penny by itself may not seem like much. However, saving over time, they accumulate and you are wealthier for the wait. In fact, achieving anything of value takes time and effort. Some people refer to it as delayed gratification. We need to work deliberately and diligently to reach our goals. It is a formula that never fails. Small, incremental successes equal richer, greater rewards. Yet, it remains difficult for people to do the little things that will eventually lead to greater dreams. Focus becomes blurred and doing the right thing dissipates while doing something simple dominates. This is where our integrity is challenged. We must be honest and true to ourselves in all actions."

Paul identified with what the old man was saying. He remembered how just that morning he had, once again, decided not to go for that morning jog. Then his thoughts raced to the speech he was neglecting. He had not given the subject much profound thought and was feeling uncomfortable with his lack of commitment. Trying to dispel the haunting intrusion, he once again tried to make light of the conversation. "A penny for your thoughts!" Paul enthusiastically blurted out.

"Certainly," the old man calmly replied. "In fact, I have a few of them. "First of all, allow me to state that 'thoughts are things.' It refers back to our discussion last week when we discussed our attitudes and how we perceive things. Additionally, and if I may quote from the stately gentleman whose profile graces this coin, "most people are about as happy as they make up their minds to be." Now, let me summarize Keith Harrell, who said it best in a nutshell, "attitude is everything." Simply said, again, by Mr. Franklin, "While we may not be able to control all that happens to us, we can control what happens inside us."

At this point the old man paused as if to place more emphasis on what he was continuing to say. "Listen closely, for here is something I wish you to understand. When situations do not always turn out how we had wished or planned, it is very easy for us to condemn, criticize and complain. Condemnation, because we believe that as an individual, we are righteous and others are filled with fault. Criticism, because we judge ourselves to be fair and others unjust. And complainers, because we consider ourselves to be cheated while others are blessed. There is no integrity nor moral compass in any of those thoughts. What we should do is exercise restraint. I am not saying to being emotionless but, to stop and think about how we are to react to different circumstances. Our thoughtless responses, although genuinely unintentional and not meant to inflict hurt, may brand us like a tattoo. This label then becomes difficult to erase. Conversely, when we are in control of our emotions, we are in control of ourselves. We refrain from allowing life's tumultuous roller coaster ride of ups and downs affect us. We should choose to remain straight and steady, like at the beginning of that wild amusement park ride."

Raising the penny once again, he referred to Abraham Lincoln. "I believe that our great President embodied that principle. He had the courage to stand up for what he believed was right in the face of constant scrutiny. He did not waver, although scores of doubters questioned his motives and abilities. He remained steadfast, sturdy and strong like a seasoned oak tree. This, in turn, defined his character as well as this great country of ours. Perhaps, this is what he was referring to when he stated that . . . "character is like a tree and reputation like its shadow. The shadow is what we think of it; the tree is the real thing."

At that moment, Paul instinctively glanced down to look at his own shadow. It was virtually nonexistent and took him by surprise. He suddenly felt the sting of the words the old man was speaking and pondered his own rectitude. Paul kicked at the ground, shuffled his feet, and flapped his arms. Try as he may, he could still only see a small representation of himself mirroring back at him. He forgot it was noon.

The old man sensing Paul's anxiety, philosophically reassured him. "Lad, do not be alarmed. Your star is directly overhead. As your days progress, so will your reputation. Be sure your character grows in the direction you choose, for it will magnify as you head into sunset."

Paul, speechless, looked up to see the old man contentedly smiling at him. A sarcastic reply seemed definitely out of line. Paul looked back down ashamedly, for the rude way in which he had treated the old man in the short time he had known him. Through misty eyes he looked back up to the old man.

"Remember," the old man encouraged, "it will take time." He then lifted his arms and gestured to a grove of trees in the distance as if they were his audience. "Look at those trees. They stand tall - as brothers in arms. One, they are but a soldier; together, a fortress. Be true to yourself, and others will be true to you."

Then the old man tightly grasped the penny and nestled it deeply into the right front pocket of his trousers. He nodded to Paul, turned and slowly ambled toward the forestry retreat. Soon he camouflaged out of sight.

Paul was dumbfounded. He looked down again and could see a slight shadow of himself attempting to cast away from his frame. Now rather than thinking of who the old man was, he was beginning to question himself. What kind of a person was he? What kind of person did he want to be? Remembering his chores, he began shuffling his way back home. The collie remained, basking in the noonday sun.

That night as Paul lay in his bed, he could not help but relive the events he experienced with the old man that day. *The penny. The trees. The names. Of course, he knew who Abraham Lincoln and Benjamin Franklin were. But who were these guys named Harrell and Frankl?* He vowed to someday find out.

Before Paul drifted off to sleep, one thought occupied his mind. *Did he pass the test?* The old man never said.

PERSEVERANCE

Little things were bothering Paul. It seemed as if continual nuisances were combining forces and battling him. The more he thought about them, the worse they became. He was not making mountains out of mole hills, the moles were making mountains where he wanted to walk. It did not help matters that his speech deadline was now only eight weeks away. Everything seemed to be attacking him at once. Paul decided to make a list of what was troubling him.

Contemplating, he scanned his bedroom. There before his eyes was the first culprit. Still unmade, the linens and covers lay in a heap in the middle of his bed. Making the bed was a simple two minute task that Paul absolutely abhorred. He often wondered how many steps it would take to embed a horseshoe path from one pillow, down the side, around the end, back up the other side and to the other pillow. He often entertained the idea of not even making his bed in the morning but again, being somewhat of a perfectionist, Paul at least tried to do the right thing. Plus, it always felt better crawling under neatly made crisp covers than dragging wrinkled blankets across his body as he got into bed at night.

Paul could hear the muffled sounds of his family in the kitchen. This prompted him to pencil in entry number two on his 'un-wish' list. He was responsible for washing, drying and returning the evening dinner dishes to the cupboards. He reasoned this chore would not be so bad if only they owned an automatic dishwasher. The debatable topic with his parents was always quashed by their views that the money used to purchase the appliance could be put to better use elsewhere. Plus they added, it helped develop character. That reason never really convinced Paul.

Feeling somewhat restless, Paul stood up from his desk and walked over to look out the window. There was item number three. He had to mow the lawn this weekend. As he relived the routine in his mind, he became more and more apprehensive. The endless repetition of pushing an aged 20" lawn mower over one-half acre of luscious lawn did not appeal to him at all. To add salt to the wound, it always seemed whenever he was mowing in the hot sun his neighbor was comfortably seated on their riding lawnmower cutting 36" swaths. In fact, they even had a gas trimmer to edge the house, sidewalk and wayward weeds that presided in the ditch. He was relegated to his hands and knees while trimming with a pair of hand shears. Paul rationalized unfairness.

Frustrated, he turned his back to the window only to gaze at his laundry basket that was partially hidden in his clothes closet. There, a mound of dirty laundry greeted him. Although this was not as repetitive as the others, he still had his disdain for doing it. So against his mother's wishes, he concocted shortcuts. He figured blue jeans were fine to wear two or three times before they needed to be washed. Since nobody could see them, two pair of socks were sufficient. One pair would be used for the week, the other for the weekend. The shirts Paul wore were strictly pullover so he could cram them in his dresser drawer after he retrieved them from the dryer. He had no patience for hangers. Ironing was out of the question. Whenever he attempted pressing his shirts for a somewhat formal event, the creases never ended up where they were supposed to and wrinkles seemed to reappear after he thought he was finished. Overall, ironing was just too much stress.

Paul wrote the numeral five on his paper and next to it wrote the word 'dusting.' How he loathed dusting. Once again, it would not be so bad except he could not quite grasp where the fine particles of pollution came from and the fact there were so many knickknacks in the house. Instead of a clean sweep of polish over an empty bookshelf, every individual deity had to be filth free. Every week, consumed with aggravation, he vowed never to purchase porcelain products. The only positive was the room did smell fresh after using the cleaner. But hey, he thought, he could just spray the whole room and let the fine mist settle over the objectless area.

Paul wrote the word 'homework' on his list. Although this was not as prevalent as the other items, it always lurked in the shadows and was a necessity to complete. For reasons he could not understand, there was particularly more this week. With just over a month remaining before graduation, what more could possibly be that important that he would need to know to carry him through the next phase of his life? Still, being the person he was, Paul felt he was personally obligated to do his best until the very end.

The final entry, he concluded, would be how he spent his evenings. Sure enough, he enjoyed not having to do anything but when there wasn't anything to do, he was trapped in boredom. The same television programs and video games had lost his interest. His collection of word game puzzles were solved. Although he enjoyed music, it did not hold his attention span long. He was tired of hanging out with friends when they also had nothing planned. Paul felt he was ready for the next chapter in his life. It was already late afternoon. He would contemplate it today at a visit to Sunny View Park.

Paul hardly noticed that through his daydreaming, he had already passed 'The Professor' and was about to embark upon an area of the park designated as a toddler's play area. Mothers and fathers would bring their children to this section so the little daredevils could expend their energy and enjoy just being a kid. Their interactions with playmates of the same age group provided education while still having fun. To the three year old, the four step plastic slide was a mountain to scale. The plastic cubes were labyrinths to explore. The sandboxes with all the spoons, forks, and buckets were laboratories to create and develop the most recent of scientific discoveries. In the mind of a child, imagination is endless, challenges are welcomed entertainment and nothing is impossible.

As Paul scanned the playground, his eyes bestowed upon an uncommon sight. Away in the distance sitting on the corner supports of a worn sandbox, was the crouched frame of a grandfatherly figure. At the opposite diagonal, a dog sat sphinx-perched as it absorbed the site and sounds of the children. Paul recognized once again, the old man and collie appeared to be waiting for him.

Paul continued toward the sandbox until he came upon their reserved repose. There he found the old man looking down, his body faced into the square of the sandbox with his elbows resting on his knees. His crumpled pant legs were soiled with sand as if he had been crawling in the sandbox himself. His hands, appearing damp and discolored, were tightly clasped with the tops of his interwoven fingers supporting his chin. His gaze intently at the ground, reminded Paul of their lessons about the penny. The collie recognizing Paul, greeted him with an uncharacteristic up and down wagging of his tail.

"I should have guessed I would find you here today," Paul greeted as he looked down at the old man.

The old man continued his silent stare into the dirt. Paul, somewhat taken aback by his inattentiveness, surveyed the ground himself. Inside, the sand had been overrun by random shoots of grass. Against the boards, weeds had begun to claim the territory. Scattered throughout, the sand had dissolved into the earth leaving hard, bare dirt as its base. Surrounding the sandbox was the answer to the errant sand. It looked as if it had been purposely scattered. Paul reasoned that uninvited guests had a sand fight and he and the old man were witnesses to their fists full of munitions.

Continuing his gaze, he finally spoke, "And how is your weekend faring, lad?"

Shuffling meekly forward with his hands in his jean pockets, Paul shrugged his shoulders while softly replying, "All right, I guess. It's like I have a lot of work, though, and not much time to do it. In fact, sometimes it seems that all I ever do is work or that I have to do something that I really don't want to." It felt good to express his feelings to someone who seemed to care. He repeated, "There's always something else to do and never time to do what I want."

The old man lifted his head and looked questionably at Paul. Squinting and in a barely audible tone, he questioned, "Oh?"

"Yeah," Paul quickly shot back. "And the stuff I do never really accomplishes anything . . . anything of value anyway. Always busy stuff. Do this, clean that, make this, fix that. It never ends. And I'm only seventeen years old. Bor-ing."

The old man's eyebrows lifted at Paul's outburst. Then the squint in his eyes tightened as he scrutinized and peered at Paul. Finally, after what seemed like hours, the old man counseled Paul. "You, my friend, have to rearrange your thinking. If you can swindle your thoughts into believing that you are hard pressed for man's most precious commodity, time, then you are only - to yourself - a fool. And to expect me to extend sympathy to a soul who lollygags when proper decision is more important, I refuse. You realize, do you not, that idle hands are the devil's workshop? It is when we have time we do not know how to fulfill that trouble finds us."

His immediate rebuttal caught Paul by surprise. He had already forgotten their first lesson concerning everything 'mattering.' Paul prepared himself. He knew he was now going to receive a lesson similar to that of a father lecturing advice to an ungovernable son. He found himself slowly enunciating each word, "I - guess - it's - not - as - bad - as - I - make - it - sound." His apology rang hollow. It was too late to retract what he rambled on about earlier which was directed more at self-pity than self-enlightenment.

The old man's glare softened and he lowered his head. He gestured towards an accompanying corner of the sandbox, "Like the shot arrow, we

28

can never retrieve the spoken word. However, please, have a seat."

Obediently, Paul submitted to the diagonal slat of wood. Sitting with his knees bent, back erect and hands neatly cupped in his lap, he was ready for his lesson. Class was in session.

The old man began in his now familiar measured methodical tone, "It is not so bad to be busy as long as we are not busy just for the sake of it. We need to have a plan and work to achieve that plan. Our goals must be realized, but we must remain flexible enough to readjust our course as needs arise." Then slightly raising his eyebrows, he asked, "I would infer that you are not familiar with Parkinson's Law?" Meekly, Paul shook his head to reaffirm the old man's supposition.

The old man continued, "Parkinson's Law is a cynical statement that says work will expand so as to fill the time available for its completion. In other words, let us not drag a project out just to occupy an allotted period of time, when actually we would be able to accomplish more. It, in a sense, also involves what we have spoken about earlier - integrity. Now, observe below." As he finished his definition, he pointed to the dirt as if his fingers were following quick, erratic movements.

Paul did as the old man requested and tried to follow the zigzagging motions. Not exactly comprehending what he was referring to, he gave up in exasperation. "What do you mean? I don't see anything."

"Closer . . . to the ground," as the old man continued his aim.

Paul leaned forward and upon closer inspection could see ants busily scurrying about the inside of the sandbox. First, he saw only a few. Then as he focused, more would appear. It reminded him of when he would look up into the evening sky. Initially, only one or two stars would be visible but as his eyes adjusted, more would magically manifest in his peripheral vision. Paul, somewhat hypnotized, looked up and absorbed a panoramic view of the area. "I have never realized all that confusion going on down there. And to think that this is happening all over this park, parks in other cities, states, and different countries all over the world." Smiling, he returned his eyes to the old man. A look of satisfaction developed over his face as if he had just discovered the meaning of life.

Sensing this, the old man grinned slightly, "Yes, it does appear to be disorientation but their social structure runs much deeper than that. They, possibly inhabiting the earth for perhaps one hundred million years, are very much like human beings. We have more in common with this highly socialized insect than what appears. They obviously seem to be on every part of this earth. In fact, the only regions where they do not exist are at very high altitudes and the polar regions of the world. They also come in many different sizes, shapes and colors. Some even live in extended families. Indeed, they are very much like us. Most interesting however, is comparing our work ethics. In the ant population, we have learned that they have somewhat of a caste system. Basically, each individual has a specific chore to perform. Whether it is a worker ant, soldier ant or harvester ant . . . it is ordained. This is even true for its queen. Likewise, in the human culture there is also evidence of this. As certain family generations evolve, many times we seem to follow in our ancestors' footsteps. We sometimes accept our fate whether it be royalty or poverty. But, as we know, this does not have to be so. Additionally, within the worker population of this insect species, there are predestined individual differences. Some are more energetic than others, some sluggish, and others who are more intense at different times of the day. Once again, very much like their human counterparts. As a whole, they are highly successful . . . just like us. It is their dedication to their work ethic that is so commendable. Each individual is genetically assigned to particular tasks and they perform them with seemingly no interruption. They are extremely focused. If there is a momentary distraction, it is not long before the insect regains its purpose. In contrast, take a person who is not focused. Some chores seem like forever for that person to complete. It reminds me of a quote by Henry David Thoreau, 'It is not enough to be busy. So are the ants. The question is: What are we busy about?' Again, it is all about work ethic. Many times, some people devote so much time avoiding the task that needs to be completed, that they could have finished it in half the time if they would have just had the initiative to do so. It also reminds me of the Roman poet Horace . . . 'He who has begun has half done. Dare to be wise; begin.' Surely, we all have periods when our motivation seems to wane somewhat. However, it is not fueled by instinct. Reason may determine our motivation for our purpose."

Then, pausing for effect, the old man asked, "Did it ever occur to you that certain people seem to get all the luck?"

Paul had thought about this before and felt this was something that he and the old man could finally agree upon. "Does it ever! It always seems that other kids are getting all the breaks and getting by me, while I struggle just to get by. Yeah, man, are they ever lucky!"

A sympathetic smile grew on the old man's face. "Quoting Roman

Stoic philosopher Seneca, he stated 'luck is what happens when preparation meets opportunity.' It is such a simple concept; yet, many refuse to accept it. They hold on to the hope that their aspirations will be a divine bequeathal. One must realize that you must work hard to achieve your goals."

"But," Paul was quick to add, "what about those who work hard and always seem to fall just a little bit short all the time? They never seem to get anywhere and always end up sad, frustrated and dejected."

A look of enlightenment suddenly appeared on the old man's face. He raised his eyebrows and just as quickly replied, "Whether they are aware of it or not, they are learning one of life's more valuable lessons. That is, we need to overcome our challenges in order to succeed. Obstacles are placed in our path to success which are designed to help us grow, develop character and persevere. I shall borrow part of a quote from Sir Winston Churchill, "Never give in. Never give in. Never; never; never; never . . .""

Then, with his right hand, the old man reached down to where there were no ants and scooped up a fistful of sand. In an almost scolding manner, he shook it in front of Paul's face. "We must hold on to our dreams." Tightening ever stronger, he continued. "They mold our future." Without any hesitation, he opened his hand to reveal the kneaded mass. "Or," he melancholically said as he scooped up more sand in his left hand and let it drift through his fingers, "they will simply slip away."

As the old man dropped the clump of sand he methodically wiped his hands. Paul looked back down at the ants and began introspective thought. He witnessed the commitment these insects shared with each other and how they performed in unison for their survival. He noted their perseverance, dedication and order. His mind began to wander as he thought about the nighttime sky and the many constellations he knew. He remembered how the asteroids, planets and galaxies revolved in relation to each other. There was order in this, too.

Paul looked at the old man and pointed to the sky. "At night," he said, "there are millions of stars out there and each one of them is tied to the other in some way or fashion. It's kind of like those ants except in a much bigger way."

"Your insight is commendable lad," the old man said. "However, you're numbers are a tad off. Actually, the count of stars in the universe is well into the billions. In fact," he added as he once again scooped up another hand full of the sandbox dirt, "if you were to put it in perspective, all of the grains of sand on all the beaches of our world is how many celestial bodies we have spinning about us."

In amazement Paul enthusiastically added, "It's almost like it's . . . endless."

"Yes, son . . . limitless." The old man paused, looked towards the sky and back at Paul again. "Limitless," he repeated. "Now, let us review. Please recall the time we spoke about children and of what they believe that they can and cannot do. Limitless. Again, think about their attitude as they go about a new venture . . . immediately and with persistence. They harbor no boundaries, just as in outer space. Their dreams are endless and their horizons are unrestricted. But, sadly, as some grow into adulthood, they also mimic characteristics of heavenly bodies. People fall into a pattern of daily mundane events which is in the safety zone of their familiarity. It is comparable to routine and order. Surely, we may alter minor events as they arise. But, as grown individuals, many resign to a life of complacency in their comfort zones. Many dream of something exciting and different. But, again, few ever try. Of those that do try as in a New Year resolution, even fewer succeed. It is easier to rationalize not fulfilling a commitment rather than stretching ourselves to succeed. Once again, words of wisdom from Mr. Thoreau . . . 'Most men lead lives of quiet desperation and go to the grave with the song still in them.'"

Paul summarized, "So, sir, what you are saying is that with the right attitude, living with integrity, being persistent and persevering through setbacks we can accomplish far more than we ever dreamed?"

The familiar contented smile once again developed on the old man's face. In fact, it resembled the look on Mr. Sain's face when a student had discovered the answer to a difficult question. "They are the commendable first steps in the journey of life. In fact, there is a quote I wish to interject which is attributed to Chinese philosopher Lao Tzu, which signifies this. He said, "A journey of a thousand miles begins with a single step."

Paul lowered his gaze and fixed it once again upon the sand below. He remembered different events in his life where he had shortchanged himself by his own doubts, fears and lack of self-confidence. Then looking up, he began to confide in the old man two stories he had never told anyone before.

"You know," Paul revealed, "there have been a couple of times that I can remember when I started a journey, but didn't quite finish it."

"Oh?" the old man questioned, encouraging Paul to go on.

"Yeah. The first time was when I was in seventh grade. A friend of mine talked me into rehearsing for the school play. I was always pretty good at reading, so I thought I would try for a part. I didn't want a very big role, so I read for a more minor character, not actually believing I would win. Well, I was awarded the part. But, not mentally ready to accept the responsibility and being very shy, I started to question my abilities to perform adequately. As a result, I decided not to participate in the program. In fact, my insecurities were so severe that I didn't even have the decency to inform the director that I was going to quit. I concocted a half-truth about why I could not be in the performance and had a fellow student inform the teacher for me. I still feel kind of bad about it."

The old man empathizing with Paul asked, "Would you do anything different if you had the opportunity to do something similar, again?"

Paul pursed his lips, thought for a minute and confessed, "I'm not sure that I really enjoy acting but I would try to realize if I had another chance, I would just try to do my best. I would try to understand that whenever anyone tries something new it is only natural that they are somewhat unsure of themselves. Everybody has to start somewhere and nobody is perfect. Nobody really wants to see somebody else fail. Having fun and learning are most important."

The old man nodded in agreement, "I could not have stated it better. Please, continue."

"Well, the second time happened when I was in the ninth grade," Paul recalled. "When I was in grade school, I was always a pretty good baseball player. I played the infield position of shortstop. So, it was only natural I would continue to play as I got older. I was aware there would be more competition in the ninth grade because of different schools combining into one. Anyway, my family was planning a vacation and I used that as an excuse not to try out. Well, the coach found out from the other players I was going to be on vacation and he even said that I could have my own personal try out with him - and to get the message to me. Although they did, I refused the offer. I had already talked myself into believing that I was not good enough. In reality, I was afraid of the increased competition and the possibility of failure. Today, I still wonder if I would have been good enough. If I had tried a little harder, what more might I have done?"

"And the lesson?" the old man prodded.

"I know, now," replied Paul, "that the fear of failure is unwarranted. We can only get better by challenging ourselves to try to improve. It is kind of like going outside of your safety zone and accomplishing something that you thought you couldn't."

"Perfect!" the old man uncharacteristically shouted. Then after composing himself added, "You realize, do you not, that the acronym for fear is 'false evidence appears real.'"

Paul, reciting the letters in his head, cracked a smile and repeated slowly, "F. E. A. R. Fear. False evidence appears real."

Somberness developed into the old man's eyes. "Most certainly, you have had some victories through the years that have made you feel confident and reassured. We must not deemphasize our successes. Please, acquaint with me a few stories."

Paul's mind raced as he tried to recall events that made him feel optimistic about himself. Since he had just finished talking about baseball, it was the first thing that he thought about. "Okay," he relinquished, "I do remember something good that happened pertaining to baseball."

"Fine," the old man replied. "Share that with me."

"Oh, it was back when I was about twelve or thirteen years old," Paul started, "and our Little League baseball team - we were in second place - was playing against the first place team. Anyway, it was our turn to be in the outfield. Well, one of their best players was the first person to bat that inning. He batted left handed, so naturally everybody on the infield moved a little to their left to accommodate where we thought he might hit the baseball. Basically, this left a larger gap between my position, shortstop and third base. All of us were on our toes trying to play the best defense we could. I don't remember exactly how many pitches were thrown to him but he connected solidly on one of them. I can still hear the crack of the bat. Then all of a sudden, I could see the ball whizzing toward me. He had smacked it so powerfully that the speeding line drive was veering away from me and headed toward the wide open gap that we created trying to defend against him. If the ball made it past me, he would have had a homerun for sure because the outfield made the same shift. To the crowd's disbelief, I instinctively stretched my left arm across the front of my body and snagged the ball out of the air. The ball instantly landed securely in my glove. My teammates congratulated me, but the other team said I was just lucky."

"Wonderful!" the old man exclaimed. "Hard work, preparedness and opportunity!"

"Wait, I'm not finished," Paul enthusiastically added. "Their next batter hit a pop up fly and I caught it to make him out, too."

"Two for two," the old man smiled. "Stupendous!"

"No, three for three," Paul corrected. "The third batter dribbled a ground ball to me. I fielded it and threw him out at first base. The inning was over and I made all three put outs!"

"Marvelous work young man," the old man cheered. "Now, relating that to what we have been discussing, what have you learned about that?"

"Hmm," Paul thought. "I guess I was ready when the time came because I practiced and played so much."

"Precisely," the old man agreed. "Listen to what you just said. Your practice was actually play. You enjoyed it. Additionally, as far as being lucky, I would have to disagree. Once again, your preparedness was met with opportunity."

"Hey, I guess you're right." Paul was starting to feel pretty positive and good about himself.

The old man egged Paul on, "Tell me another."

Paul pensively lifted his right hand to his face and stroked his chin. "When I was about the same age, I spent a lot of my summer vacations at the local swimming pool. Rather than always being in the water, I devoted most of my time to diving off the one meter and three meter boards. My friends and I would constantly challenge each other to perform different acrobatics from the diving boards to see who could do them best. One particular such dive was called a 'gainer.' This is when a diver jumps off the diving board from a forward position but then propels himself into a backward somersault and ends up feet first in the water facing away from the board. It is a fancy dive that amateurs don't try very often. But, it's relatively safe because the bottoms of your feet break the surface of the water and allow for a smoother entrance into the pool. A variation of that dive is called a 'half gainer.' A half gainer is when the diver jumps off the front of the diving board and only does a half backward somersault and dives headfirst into the water facing the board. The only thing the diver has to break the surface of the water are his hands in front of his head, so it's a little more dangerous. If you did not flip backward far enough as you arched your back, you did what we called a back smacker. If you over compensated, you would do a belly flop. Those are the two main reasons why we did that dive off the lower diving board. If we messed up, it didn't sting as bad."

Paul continued, "One day, between swimming sessions, we dared each other to do a half gainer from the high dive. It was the usual peer pressure bantering that teenagers do to try to get somebody to do something first. The most prominent thing I remember being said was that if I tried first, others would follow my lead. Well, I took the challenge. I can remember it happening like it was yesterday. I was the first one in the fenced in swimming area while the others waited and watched outside. I reasoned that if I failed at my attempt, there wouldn't be as many people to laugh at me. Anyway, after the climb up the ladder, I found myself slowly walking the plank to its edge. Looking down to my right, I heard them continue to dare me, as well as their convictions that I was not going to go through with it. I stood there, replaying the motions of the dive in my head and contemplating the adjustments I would have to make to perform the feat. Then, possessed, I leaped out over the open water. I honestly don't know what happened next. The only thing I remember is slicing the water with my hands pointed to break my entrance into the pool. As I surfaced from the depths of the water, I recall scrutinizing any pain from different parts of my body. There was none. I had completed the dive!"

The old man appeared delighted. "Splashing!" he said. "You accomplished more than just a dive. With a positive attitude you conquered your fear, persisted through doubt, persevered through the challenge, and ultimately did what you said you were going to. In effect, establishing integrity."

"I did all that?" Paul asked.

"And more," the old man added. "You developed self-confidence which would serve to be your ally in future goals."

Paul's thoughts once again began retracing other accomplishments he had achieved. "There was the time I played in the second game of a Junior Varsity double header baseball game and got two hits. In that same game, my teammate and I successfully completed a double play. Also, in an intramural basketball game, I remember how I was scoring baskets from far away even before there was an established 3-point arc. In one of my classes, I remember how I earned enough points to pass the class with an 'A' average without even having to take the final exam."

"This is good what we have done here today," the old man concluded. "Even though we are aware of some of our misgivings, we can be sure that we have as many, if not more, victories. It is through these triumphs that we must disregard negatives in our past and focus on positives for the future. No more pessimism, always optimism."

Paul felt elated. He was excited and determined to accomplish and achieve even more in his life. "Let's talk about some more stuff," he encouraged the old man.

"Another time. We had a late start today and dusk is beginning to fall," the old man replied.

The old man strolled over to the collie who had remained steadfast through the conversation. It was as if he, too, was absorbing the lessons. His obedience was admirable. The old man stooped down, patted the dog on the head and adjusted his topcoat as he rose. With a reaffirming, "You are one fine friend," turned to walk away. Before he ambled out of sight, he looked back to Paul one more time. "Paul, we will meet, again." With a two finger salute to his forehead, the old man nodded his head as he disappeared behind a grove of trees.

Paul stood up and turned to look at the collie. As if on cue, the dog steadily raised himself up. His tags rattled as he shook himself to loosen his tightened muscles. Slowly, he nudged against Paul's legs and also began to walk away.

As Paul watched him leave, he saw the dog head towards a fence that divided a neighborhood from Sunny View Park. Feeling somewhat responsible for the safety of the animal, Paul wanted to be certain that he would find his way home. Reaching the fence, the dog disappeared behind overgrown clinging vines. Paul figured there was a hidden opening that must have allowed the collie to enter the backyard to one of the houses. Then the silhouette of the dog reappeared as he made his way to a back porch. After a few quick barks, Paul heard the opening of a door, muffled voices, and the door shutting. Paul felt comfortable the dog was now safely inside his master's house. Paul turned to head home.

Lying in bed that night, Paul once again replayed the events of the afternoon in his head. *Who was this nameless old man that always seemed to appear lately whenever he went to the park?* Next time, he would be determined to ask him his name because the old man did say that they would meet again. Paul shut his eyes, but opened them back up just as quickly. Somewhat startled he wondered, *how did the old man know his name was Paul?* He had never told him.

Easter weekend had arrived. This year it occurred later in the month of April than normally. Seasonally, it symbolized the Earth was warming and summer was preparing to replace spring. For Paul, it meant that he was down to about six weeks before he was required to have his assignment completed. As was becoming commonplace, he elected to do his chores on Saturday and go to Sunny View Park on Sunday. Besides, going to the park on Easter Sunday was a tradition he had been following for as long as he could remember.

As Paul visited the park, he recalled how excited he always was on this day. The baseball diamond where he now stood served as a reminder of the fun he had here. His conversations with the old man made it all the more memorable. This field also served as the location where the annual Easter egg hunts were held. Actually, the word 'hunt' was a misnomer. The 'hidden' eggs were spread out in plain view and the hunt was really just a race to see who could collect the most. Plus, the eggs were the pastel colored plastic kind that would unscrew so a treat could be placed inside. The local businesses would donate trinket gifts from their shops and offer them as prizes in the plastic orbs.

Every year the routine was the same. Groups of children would be divided into similar age groups, and at a predetermined signal, they would scamper around the area to scoop up the eggs. The youngest groups, which included the parents strolling their infants, would start at 10:00 a.m. By noontime, the final group which consisted of nine and ten year olds, were finishing.

The Easter egg hunt had ended and the last group was mingling on the baseball diamond. Paul continued to survey the field because sometimes an errant egg would sit partially hidden in a clump of grass. He could see that all were found and he was witness to another successful Easter egg hunt in Lincoln. As he scanned the area, however, he noticed the collie stoically sitting on the far end of the baseball diamond. Scoping on the dog, Paul deduced from the animal's focus that he was watching someone in the field. Paul continued to study and it soon became apparent the collie was isolating one particular younger boy.

Confirming his suspicions, Paul noticed the slightly built, bespectacled brown haired boy suddenly sprint toward the dog. The collie, obviously unable to contain his excitement, stood up and happily began barking while frantically wagging his tail in that uncharacteristic up and down motion. His hind quarters wiggled from side to side as his front paws pounded the ground. Paul reasoned that he had finally solved the mystery of the dog's owner.

The boy quickly reached the collie, dropped to his knees, and displayed three colorful objects for the dog to inspect. Paul observed that the boy had collected a purple, green, and blue egg. The aroused collie curiously began sniffing the prizes the boy had found. He then perched his paws on the boy's lap and began earnestly licking his face, smothering him with kisses. The boy, giggling with joy, wrapped his arms around the collie's neck and hugged him with delight. Their love for each other was obvious.

Paul decided since he already somewhat knew the dog, he would go over to meet the youthful boy. As he did, he noticed another figure also heading in the same direction. From an area of the park occupied by swings, seesaws, and merry-go-rounds, the old man was trudging his way to the lad and canine reunion. After a few short minutes, the four of them converged.

"Ahoy mates," the old man saluted. His cheerful tone caught Paul off guard for he was accustomed to the old man being serene and tranquil. Perhaps, Paul thought, the usual calmness normally exhibited was reserved only for him.

Wondering if the old man was actually the boy's grandfather, Paul replied, "Hello. You were right. We are meeting, again. Is this your grandson?"

The boy answered that question quickly when he interjected, "No, that's not my grandpa, that's Captain Barnaby! Don't you think he looks like the captain of a ship?"

Before Paul could answer, the old man reached down and ruffled the boy's hair, "Timothy, my young sailor, how has thee fared, lately?"

"Look what I got," Timothy excitedly responded. He then bent down, picked up the eggs, supported them against his chest and turned back to show the old man.

"Spectacular work, Timothy," the old man congratulated. "Splendid catch."

"You two know each other, huh?" Paul confirmed.

"Of course," said the boy. "Everybody knows Captain Barnaby!"

"Absolutely," the old man agreed, "and this is first mate Timothy. We have solidified a friendship for some time now. He and his comrade make a fine team."

"That explains it," said Paul. "You've known this dog all along because you knew Timothy. I thought you believed it was kind of homeless."

"No, I am afraid I never volunteered that information," the old man confided. "I did confide that I trusted he had a home, somewhere. Of little concern. In any case, Timothy, this is Paul."

But before Timothy could answer, Paul interrupted, "Oh yeah, I was going to ask you, how did you know my name was Paul?"

"The Captain knows everything," Timothy blurted. "He even knew my name too, before I knew his. Anyway, hi." He reached up and shook Paul's hand.

"So, you're name, sir, is Barnaby. Mr. Barnaby." Paul then extended his hand because they had never been formerly introduced.

"Yes, that I am," the old man softly replied as he reached out to shake hands with Paul. "But you, as well as Timothy, may just refer to me as Barnaby. It is one of those names that can be used as a first as well as a last. And he," as the old man pointed to the collie, "he . . . is Silas."

"Yup," the boy added. "And the Captain knew his name, too, before I wanted to tell him."

"How did you come up with the name Silas, Timothy?" Paul questioned.

"Well," he answered, "my mom wanted to call him Lassie but that's more for a girl. So, we kind of switched the letters around and came up with Silas." He confidently added, "That's a boy's name."

"Almost a complete anagram," the old man educated. "Additionally," he said as he gestured to the trees which divided the park from the neighboring subdivision, "it is very appropriate for the pooch and its environment. The name 'Silas' is derived from the Greeks and refers to 'forest' or 'woods.'"

After a short pause, Paul contributed, "Wasn't there a T.V. show years ago called Lassie, about a boy and his collie?"

"Precisely," the old man commended, "and quite astonishing, all of the canines, Lassies, that starred as the lead character were actually males."

"Cool," grinned Timothy. "I told you Captain Barnaby knows

41

everything!"

"Enough trivia," the old man decided as he nodded towards Timothy, "Let us inspect your treasures."

Timothy, still clutching the eggs close to his chest, fumbled them briefly in his hands. He then held them out for the old man and Paul to see. "Look, a purple one, a green one, and a blue one."

"Those are my three favorite colors," Paul complimented. "I bet the purple one has the best prize."

"Let's see," Timothy replied as he knelt down and set them on the ground. "But I want to open the blue one first."

"As you wish," the old man smiled.

Timothy then picked up the blue Easter egg and firmly grasping each end, unscrewed the plastic oval. "Wow!" he exclaimed as he examined the contents.

Inside were three foil wrapped chocolate Easter egg candies. Mystifyingly, one was purple, the other green and the last one blue.

Timothy, building on his excitement squealed, "Weird. These are all Paul's favorite colors, again."

"Yes, quite baffling," the old man assured.

"It's not strange to me at all," Paul stated, with a slight emphasis of his earmarked sarcasm.

"Yeah, right," Timothy reasoned. "Anyway, there's one for each of us."

Timothy placed the three pieces of candy in his right hand. With his fingers outstretched and the candy nestled in the center of his palm, he politely offered Barnaby first choice. Calmly, the old man selected the green chocolate. Next, Paul obviously chose the purple candy. The last piece, blue, was for Timothy. He was happy because that was his favorite color, too.

"Thanks, Timothy," Paul said as he immediately unwrapped the bite sized morsel and promptly popped it into his mouth.

"Your generosity is noteworthy," the old man agreed as he meticulously removed the paper from the chocolate. He carefully placed the candy in his mouth and as it slowly melted added, "You reap what you sow."

"Huh?" Paul asked.

"Kindness is always repaid in full," Barnaby explained. "You get what you give."

"Told ya'," Timothy grinned, referring to the old man's expansive knowledge. He ripped the foil from the chocolate candy and in seconds, his was gone.

The old man cast his eyes back upon the ground. "Shall we next unlock the secret of the green egg?" posing the question to Timothy.

"Sure," he answered, obediently picking up the plastic object and twisting it open.

Inside this egg was another pink plastic egg. Bewildered, Timothy let the smaller egg roll out of its larger home and studied the plastic toy. After some hesitation, he pried it open. Inside he discovered what appeared to be a marble sized ball of clay. He picked out the miniature globe and gently squeezed it between his thumb and forefinger.

"What in the world is this?" he asked, hoping for a simple answer for something so strange.

"That looks like Silly Putty," Paul chimed in. "That stuff is great! I used to get that every year in my Easter basket when I was a kid. You can roll it, bounce it, stretch it, and even split it apart. I used to squash it flat and press it on faces in my comic books. Then their picture was on the Silly Putty. After that, I would pull on the different edges to stretch it and make them look goofy."

Timothy, puzzled, tested the old man, "Really?"

"Paul is quite correct, Timothy," the old man reassured. "However, allow me to add my perspective. It was originally developed as a substitute for rubber in World War II. It is quite flexible at room temperature yet as heat is applied it becomes more malleable. Conversely, in a cooler atmosphere it is more rigid. If a blunt force is abruptly applied, it will tend to break apart. And, being considered a liquid, it will conform to the shape of its container. Mysteriously, if it were placed over a hole on a table it would eventually drip thoroughly through it."

"It sounds as if it has its own behavior . . . its own personality," figured Paul.

"I concur," replied the old man. "I correlate it in this manner. Consider it to be a person facing an obstacle. When he 'warms' up to the challenge, he stretches himself beyond his limits for personal success. But, if the hard knocks of life stop him in his tracks, he breaks down cold and dejected. If this person presses himself to victory, he does not allow himself to wallow by the wayside to liquefy and mold."

After what seemed like hours of silence, Paul broke the ice by suggesting to the boy, "Hey Timothy, open the third egg."

Timothy deftly returned the putty to its shell and placed that in the empty green plastic container. Carefully placing it on the ground, he picked up the purple egg while unscrewing it to reveal its contents. Rolled up inside was a piece of paper wrapped like a miniature scroll and tied with golden string. Expecting to see a treat, the perplexed boy untied the lace, flattening the parchment and started reading, "The bearer of this document is entitled to one free book as a present from the Lincoln Library."

Enchantment spread across the old man's face. "A fabulous gift," he assured as he began to impart knowledge to his young charges. "America's first library was formed by Benjamin Franklin and some friends back in the 1700s. At that time, books were rare and expensive, being available to only the wealthy and the clergy. However, through their founding efforts, books eventually became available to all. Additionally, my young treasure hunter, the first librarian was in fact, named Louis Timothee," as he stressed the syllables Tim - o - thee.

Paul looked over to Barnaby, "Amazing. How did you know that?"

"I have spent many enjoyable hours in the company of many fine friends . . . books," the old man endorsed. "When you decide to allow them to converse with you, a dialogue to a whole new world is initiated. They will escort you to horizons never before imagined."

"Cool," the boy excitedly expressed. "I wonder what I'll choose."

"I am certain you will make a superior choice Timothy," the old man reassured. "Already you display a wisdom beyond your years."

Timothy neatly creased the coupon in half and tucked it in the right front pocket of his jeans. As he did this, he retrieved a small lunch sack that he had folded in his back left pants' pocket. He was prepared to stow whatever he found during the Easter egg hunt in the bag so it would be easier to carry. After dropping the eggs in the sack, he looked around the emptying park and suggested, "Let's go over to the playground."

Timothy then laid his bag of eggs on the ground. Paul agreed, stipulating that he could only stay for a short time because he would have to be home early for Easter dinner. Barnaby introspectively confirmed as the three proceeded on a path to their destination.

The playground was an area dedicated to a variety of engaging equipment which formed a boundary around a community drinking fountain. The neatly manicured area was inviting to both the young and elderly. As one approached, the first objects encountered were a duo of seesaws. These teeter-totters welcomed visitors as one end of their plank rested firmly on the ground. To the left of those were a set of slides. A six-step version was the choice of toddlers while its neighboring cousin boasted twelve steps for the more daring. Next to that were a trio of balance beams. Implanted firmly one foot above the ground was a ten foot long, eight inch wide board. As children safely walked the length of it, they were led to another which was three feet above the ground and six inches wide. If this could successfully be navigated, that steered them to the last beam. It was six feet above the ground and only four inches wide. A small ladder was attached to this challenge, as all three rested in cushioning mulch if anyone were to fall. A swing set occupied the area as one continued from the balance beams. Two chained flexible rubber seats hung close to the ground, while adjacent to those were two higher positioned ones. Finally, the familiar amusement ride known as the merry-go-round completed the circle. It functioned the same as the similar carnival apparatus revolving around the center post. However, instead of circus animals to sit on, five boards served as seats for eager riders. This menagerie of childhood entertainment provided fun as well as growth development.

Timothy sped ahead as Paul, the old man, and Silas approached the playground. He raced past the drinking fountain and directly toward the balance beams. In fluent stride, he mastered the lowest structure, darting across before pausing to catch his breath and ascending the second. Hugging the timber, he hoisted himself up to command the challenge. Artfully, he navigated the obstruction, leaping off at the end. After a slight hesitation, Timothy continued to the final beam. As he quickly climbed the ladder, he found himself standing ankle to ankle at the beginning of the board, contemplating.

Paul was reminded of the time when he found himself in the similar situation when he competed against a school athlete in an obstacle course race. "Do you think he'll try it," he asked Barnaby as the two were now standing nearby.

"Without a doubt," the old man convinced. "You do recollect our conversation concerning youths and their absence of fear, do you not?"

Paul and the old man dutifully watched as Timothy began his trek. Instinctively, Timothy raised his arms as he skillfully toed the board. Halfway to the end, he lost his stability as his weight began to shift.

"Balance," the old man whispered "emulate the scales of equality."

"Careful," cautioned Paul.

The old man continued to watch the boy and clarified, "Clearly, we observe the physical equilibrium of which Timothy is striving to obtain. Lest we forget, we must also achieve mental steadiness. Timothy is displaying this quality as he prepares his brief journey to completion. Collectively, as in life, one must be uniform physically and mentally, as well as emotionally and spiritually. We must not overcompensate in one area to justify lack in another. Though this discipline of oneself may be a constant challenge to attain, we are better for the effort. Prudence."

Just as the old man finished, Timothy's faltering intensified. Squatting and kneeling, bobbing and swaying, his flailing arms flapped continuously as he struggled to remain steady. Then, as if calmed by an invisible force, his stance firmed and he boldly traversed the final balance bar. Proudly, he jumped to the mulch cushioned ground and barrel rolled to his feet. Turning to Paul and Barnaby he raised his fists in the air like a prize fighter shouting, "Victory!"

Paul, grinning, shouted an approving, "Yes!" Barnaby nodding in approval, simply gestured a 'thumbs up' with both hands.

Timothy now headed for the giant slide as Barnaby suggested to Paul they have a seat on the merry-go-round. Once there, the pair looked across to see Timothy scaling the rungs of the ladder. He rapidly transcended the first few steps as his hands barely held the safety rails. He gradually slowed as he clutched the tubular metal handles tighter and tighter as he rose to the top. For a split second, he rested.

"Were you witness to that Paul?" Barnaby asked.

"I'm not sure what you mean," Paul replied, turning his head from side to side as his eyes darted across the playground. "I don't see anything."

"No, I mean Timothy. Did you follow his actions?" Barnaby continued.

"Nothing out of the ordinary to me," Paul answered. "Did he whack his shin or something?"

Figuring Paul was unaware of what he was referring to, the old man established, "No. Timothy just executed an action that many of us perform as we tackle a new project. We charge full speed ahead at the onset but just as quickly as we advance, we lose steam. Our energy and motivation become sapped and we resolve for more effortless avenues. Some even decide to quit. It appears Timothy is pondering just that. He is harboring indecision, unsure of his direction, and wondering if he should retreat or refuel. However, all is not lost. Sometimes we need to slow down, show restraint, and rethink our motives before turning back. Many times it is actually smoother when we have a designed approach. Temperance."

As Barnaby finished his correlation, Timothy regrouped and pulled himself up the final steps. Then standing on the platform he turned to the old man and Paul. While saluting he shouted, "Triumph!"

Paul waved and cheered, "Good job!"

Barnaby, gratified, looked at Paul and summed up the boy's accomplishment, "Fortitude."

After propelling himself down the slide, Timothy scampered to the swing set. Paul and Barnaby shuffled their feet to spin their carousel so they could attest to his next heroics. With the swing set right next to the merry-go-round, they had a front seat view. Soon the show began. Timothy plunked himself down into the rubber saddle of a taller swing and tightly grasped its chain link supports. Protruding his chest forcefully forward, while stretching his arms back, he initiated momentum. Leaning back, he gained impetus. Again, he replicated the motion and was soon smoothly gliding to and fro.

"Watch me go higher!" Timothy yelled, as he pumped his legs harder.

Paul smiled at the boy and turned to the old man, "I bet there's a lesson here, too. Huh, Barnaby?"

"Of course," he agreed. "But it is extremely simple."

"I bet it has something to do with determination," Paul confided.

"Correct again," Barnaby replied.

Paul observed Timothy more closely. Timothy had been working feverishly and was reaching the zenith of his forward push. As he strived for more altitude, he could see the muscles tighten in his jaw. Paul sensed the grit and grind as Timothy clenched his teeth. With squinting eyes, Timothy sucked a mouthful of air through his teeth as his hair blew back. Then, without warning, Timothy propelled himself out of the swing, landing squarely flat footed on the grass below. "Now, it's time for some water and then I have to go home," he reported as he jogged to the drinking fountain.

Meanwhile, the old man took his cane and aimed it towards the ground below the merry-go-round. Paul watched as Barnaby carved an 'X' into the sand. Looking back at Timothy, the old man asked if he would give him and Paul a hearty push before he departed. Obliging, Timothy walked to the opposite side of the merry-go-round and firmly grabbed a seat and rail. Digging his feet in, he pushed as the force began the carousel moving. Kicking harder, he soon garnered enough force to send it revolving comfortably.

"We are gracious," Barnaby quipped as he tipped his hat.

"Yeah, thanks . . . I guess," Paul added.

"Yep," Timothy answered. "Okay, I'm going, now. C'mon, Silas." Timothy ran to the end of the path where he had set his bag of eggs. Retrieving them, he turned back one more time, "See ya' later Captain Barnaby. See ya' Paul." Before long, he and Silas were out of sight.

The force Timothy provided for the old man and Paul to spin was sufficient to pass the imprinted 'X' two times. With each pass, Barnaby stabbed his cane on the ground next to it for added reinforcement. As the merry-go-round idled slowly to a stop, it magically rested in front of the mark for a third time. Paul listened as Barnaby looked up to him and began to speak.

"Henceforth, I am going to reveal to you two idioms which represent our double passing of the 'X' I have ingrained in the sand. Appropriately, as I define these, it is your choice as how to proceed with your interpretation. Do you understand?" the old man asked.

Although he was not quite positive, Paul slightly nodded his head in agreement, "Sure." Barnaby, he thought, always had a way of speaking mysteriously. Yet when his lectures were over, his communication was refreshingly clear.

The old man began, "Our brief excursion on this revolving apparatus is what prompted me to offer you this insight. There is a saying, 'what goes around comes around.' Elementarily speaking, it is karma, dealing with cause and effect. It can also be related to Sir Isaac Newton's Third Law of Motion which states, 'for every action there is an equal and opposite reaction.' What I would simply like to imply is in a humanistic approach, good action results in good results and bad action results in bad results. It may not be immediately evident . . . or observed at all. Yet, it is a belief held by many."

"That's kind of like 'you reap what you sow'," Paul remembered from their earlier discussion.

"Very good," the old man credited. He continued, "The second idea which comes to mind is that 'this too shall pass.' It is based on a story about wisdom and King Solomon. Abraham Lincoln also borrowed its reference in one of his more memorable speeches. Basically, its context expresses that in certain times and situations, our pride must be chastened. We must not overindulge ourselves with boastfulness for it will not last forever. Conversely, in unhappier times, our afflictions must be consoled. Bad times come and bad times go. We should not depress ourselves with negative feelings. We must monitor our thoughts, feelings, and deeds and maintain them in moderation."

Paul eased himself off his seat on the merry-go-round and turned to face Barnaby. "Well," he said, "the only thing we haven't talked about is the teeter-totters over there," pointing to the see saws.

"Right," Barnaby agreed. "Let us pay them a visit before we adjourn for the day."

The two walked in silence toward the weather worn boards. Paul, arriving at his end first, reached down and lifted the plank from its depression in the ground. Straddling his end, he steadied the slat and advised Barnaby to sit on the opposite end. His idea was to level the timber so each could mount safely. Barnaby securely grasped the bolted handle with one hand while bracing himself with his cane in the other. He then propped himself onto the plank sidesaddle. Paul firmly planted his feet on the ground and sat down, leveling the board.

"Care to go for a ride?" Paul sarcastically asked grinning like a Cheshire cat.

"Only slightly," Barnaby relented. "The body is not as agile as it once was."

"Just kidding," confessed Paul as he gently rocked the board three to four inches.

"If I were more youthful, we could better demonstrate my rendition of our present situation. However, we will just have to rely on lecture. It will serve us just as well."

"I'm ready," confirmed Paul.

"We have encountered the fourth and final virtue," remarked Barnaby. "This teachable moment reminds us that life presents us with ups and downs which precipitate us to question the motives of our fellow man. This forces us to level the peaks and valleys of the matter - allowing us to survey the pros and cons of circumstance. To open the locked door to judgment and cast light upon the hidden corner of darkness. And, to steady the sagacious scales of Libra, to sustain equilibrium during strife and opposition. Basically, balance for the betterment. Justice."

This was deeper in thought than what Paul had imagined the daily ups and downs of life entailed. But, he was becoming familiar with Barnaby's dissertations and had this growing feeling he was grooming him to think more profoundly. Paul reasoned that he would think more about it at some other time.

"That was a lot of interesting information today in a short period of time," Paul commented, as he backed off the seesaw while still steadily balancing the old man.

"Time can be friend or foe," Barnaby smiled. "I try to remain busy and be on its good side."

"Good idea," replied Paul. "Anyway, it's time for me to leave now, too. So, I guess I'll meet up with you . . . who knows when?"

"Soon, I'm sure," reassured Barnaby as he stepped away from the teeter-totter and let the plank drop to the ground.

Paul, momentarily reflecting, placed his hand on the end of the board that was suspended in the air. Gently, he drew down his arm to try to balance the timber. Overcompensating, it thumped to the ground. Lifting it ever so lightly, he softly raised the plank as Barnaby intently observed. Once again, the extra exertion Paul provided caused the board to drop on its opposite end. The old man looked amusingly at the board near his feet. In frustration, Paul shook his head, turned, and walked away.

Familiar with a feeling he had grown accustomed to as he departed company from the old man, Paul looked back one last time. With a contented look on his face, the old man was wedging his cane between the board and the ground. Ever so meticulously, he gingerly elevated the board inch by inch. Calculating its height, he gently removed his staff from beneath the board as it balanced perfectly parallel to the earth. The old man, quite satisfied, turned and walked away.

REFLECTION

Spring break for Lincoln High had come and gone. Along with its departure, it kidnapped the sense of urgency Paul had privately reserved to complete his speech. Spring fever was at elevated degrees and any homework assignment at all was a challenge. Paul was feeling particularly anxious this Saturday morning with only four weeks remaining before the deadline. It was as if somebody had pushed his panic button. Then an idea descended upon him. Why he had not thought of it before befuddled him. Barnaby, he reasoned, was empowered with infinite wisdom. He would innocently ask the old man what his speech topic should be.

The April showers of the past week had relented to clear blue skies of this crisp morning. Although breezy and brisk, it was bright and reminded Paul of an Aesop fable he had read as a child. It was about a contest between the North wind and the sun to see who could make a man remove his jacket. The wind, fierce and wild, blew hard and heavy while the sun hid behind a cloud. This however, only made the man clutch tighter to his cloak. Failing, the wind submitted to the sun to have opportunity. In all its glory, the brilliant sun beamed its warmth which incited the traveler to passively remove his coat. As he thought about the morals to the story, Paul also deemed it appropriate to his present situation. Persuasion is better than force and kindness is more effective than severity. He would use these intentions to try to influence Barnaby for suggestions concerning his assignment. The more he thought about it, the better he felt. He had actually related a story to a circumstance. Barnaby would be proud.

Arriving at Sunny View, Paul decided to search for the old man in areas where he had previously encountered him. There was an elderly couple resting from their morning stroll on the benches across from 'The Professor.' At the sandbox was a family of four building castles in the moist warming sand. The baseball diamond was being taken prisoner by two teams of Little Leaguers and their families for a weekend tournament. The playground was host to the children of those families. Determined, Paul resolved to comb the entire park.

Paul's wandering led him to the furthest area of Sunny View Park. Being at the opposite end of the entrance, the general public did not visit this section often. In Paul's opinion, it was more an area of refuge than recreation. Nevertheless, being on a mission, he wanted to investigate all possibilities.

A small brook meandered its way through the uneven terrain. This provided somewhat of a boundary as it shadowed a cyclone fence enclosing Sunny View. From the recent rains and melting snow, the area resembled a lush green carpet. Long blades of grasses swayed in the gentle breeze concealing pockets of pooled water. In some areas, it was somewhat of a marsh that was home to cattails and errant, overgrown weeds. As Paul tip-toed throughout the area, he was careful not to soak his feet in the obscured puddles.

Surveying the area, Paul was fascinated by a mammoth oak tree. Solitarily it stood, its massive base majestically supporting an array of towering branches above him. It was a perfect structure demanding attention from anything within its sight.

"Reach. Stretch. Extend." A voice came seemingly from out of nowhere.

Paul instantly recognized the tone as Barnaby's. But, the old man was nowhere to be seen. "Is that you Barnaby?" Paul tried to verify as his eyes scouted the area.

"And who were you expecting, my friend?" came the reply as the old man appeared from behind the massive girth of the tree.

"Barnaby," Paul exclaimed. "I was hoping to find you, today. There's something I wanted to talk to you about. I've got something to ask you."

The old man revealed, in anticipation, a sly smile that let Paul know the old man already realized what he was going to request. Yet, respectfully, Barnaby appeared surprised, "Oh?"

"You probably already know, but I'm going to ask you anyway," Paul said. "I need your advice . . . a suggestion." Paul then explained, detailing the events of the past six weeks when he was first assigned his speech.

The old man listened politely. After Paul finished, Barnaby spoke, "I am going to repeat my salutation from earlier. Reach . . . stretch . . . extend."

"What do you mean?" Paul earnestly asked.

Barnaby stepped toward Paul and with his free hand familiarly wrapped it around Paul's forearm. Then, using his cane as a lead, guided him out from under the tree. There they had a better view of the commanding presence of the mighty oak.

"Judging from the size of the trunk of this prized specimen, I would have to say it is close to 250 years old. That tells me it took root about the same time as the beginning of this great nation. Look at the grace it has earned. Nevertheless, its life commenced as a single acorn among thousands. Conditions were favorable as it reposed in its surroundings. Buried, it germinated, struggled upward, and broke through the surface of the earth. In its early years it sprouted into a sapling. As time progressed, it grew strength and supported itself with a solid root system to weather wind, storms, and drought. As years passed, it developed into what it is today. It has matured into a monument spreading its acorns for new expansion. How did this happen? It reached. It stretched. It extended. The budding of its branches gave opportunity for new growth, just as fresh ideas gave new birth to our developing country."

"So, what does this have to do with my speech?" Paul asked without trying to be snide.

"Fresh ideas," the old man repeated. "Fresh thoughts. Your thoughts. Remember from earlier," he emphasized, "thoughts are things. Inspire. They must be planted in your own soil. Then, they must be allowed to grow in your personal environment. You have to develop a base . . . a strong foundation. Through time, your thoughts will branch out through others, and their ideas will flourish. Like the oak spreading its acorns for more trees, your ideas will be sown to others for better living. If one idea allows for another to grow, it will serve . . . as does the mighty oak." The old man paused, "You . . . must decide."

The answer Barnaby gave was not what Paul wanted to hear. However, he realized what the old man said was correct. "I guess you're right Barnaby. I'll try to think of something on my own."

"Remember, be true to yourself," Barnaby advised. Moving his hand from Paul's arm to his wrist the mentor added, "Come, follow me."

The old man led Paul to the creek that bordered the fence. Peering at the lazily streaming water, it seemed Barnaby was searching for something that was perhaps hidden on the banks. Paul smiled to himself as he thought about the silver penny and the ants. *Was there something out here buried in the grass?* He wondered. He tagged along, still being steered by the old man.

Barnaby slowed as if he found what he was searching for and crept to the edge of the stream. Inching closer, he motioned for Paul to do the same. The two of them stood as they stared at a segregated pool of undisturbed water. Barnaby knelt on the cushioning overgrown grasses that bordered the creek, pulling Paul with him. Copying the old man, Paul craned his neck to see what was in the pond.

Almost chuckling Paul asked, "What are you looking at, Barnaby?"

"You," the old man succinctly replied.

Paul studied the water. The sun was casting a perfect reflection onto the glistening pooled reservoir. It was as if they were looking into a mirror. He looked up at Barnaby and tried to contain his humor. "Why are you looking at me down in the water when you can look at me up here?"

The old man was undeterred by Paul's slight sarcasm. "I was wondering, if you see the same person as I?"

Suddenly Paul felt uncomfortable. Barnaby had set the stage for introspection and Paul was disrespecting him. "I'm not sure I know what you mean Barnaby," Paul confessed trying to assuage the atmosphere.

Without taking his eyes from the creek the old man continued. "Look back down and take a careful inspection of yourself. Do you observe the person that you are . . . that you want to be? Or, are you a product of peer pressure being someone you think others desire of you? Are you a part of the crowd or do you march to the beat of your own drum? When you go to bed at night, are you satisfied with how you lived the day and treated others? And, when you look in the mirror in the morning, are you happy with the person who is greeting you?"

Paul stared at his reflection. He thought that he was a good person. Perhaps there were some areas where he could do better. In defense, he meekly answered, "I think I try."

Sensing Paul's insecurity, Barnaby reassured him in a fatherly manner. "Paul, I know you are a very good person, indeed. You do try. What I want to impart with you is that everyone can say nicer things, do better actions and be better people. I know your intensity. Do not sacrifice it for the sake of complacency. For your speech, you must first reach inside to find what is dear to your heart. Then, stretch yourself beyond what you believe your limits to be. Finally, extend what you have found and offer it to others."

That encouragement made Paul feel better. Simultaneously, they smiled at each other as they gripped each other's hands in a firm handshake. "Thanks, Barnaby. I needed that," Paul admitted.

"Come, Paul," Barnaby coaxed as he struggled to his feet. "There is something I observed earlier I would also like you to see."

The old man led Paul back to the sturdy oak. As they approached, Barnaby guided them to a branch which supported a variety of limbs. Lifting his cane, he pointed to a smaller twig in particular. "Do you see what I am directing at?" he asked.

Paul strained his eyes, trying to see what the old man was referring to. He noticed the pupa of a monarch butterfly. "Yes, I see it now," Paul confirmed.

"Did you know," the old man began, "that as this caterpillar develops into a butterfly it goes through a great change. In its final stages, as the chrysalis is growing, the cocoon becomes quite transparent. The butterfly struggles as it tries to free itself from its self-designed encasement. As it overcomes its challenges, it is rewarded with its freedom. Paul," the old man stressed, "if at any time during this process that any assistance would be offered to the developing butterfly, it may die. It needs to overcome its hardship to strengthen its wings. It would be a disservice to that delicate insect. That is why I cannot make any suggestions for your speech. You must develop your own wings so you can fly."

Paul never knew that information about the monarch butterfly. At first he felt sad that such a small fragile creature had so much to endure. Then he felt happy that in the end it developed into something so beautiful. He realized challenges seem to test everybody and everything and that all are stronger as they overcome their obstacles. "Thanks Barnaby for your help again today. I did learn a lot."

The old man sensing his sincerity, nodded. "Paul, I cannot tell you what to do; but do what you can and to the best of your ability."

Paul turned and walked toward home as the old man disappeared behind the tree.

OPTIMISM

The first weekend of May found Paul sitting at his desk in his bedroom, gazing at a half empty glass of soda. On this early Saturday afternoon, he realized that he had less than one month remaining to create, construct, and execute a speech for Lincoln High. On the tablet before him a blank page stared back as he fidgeted with his pencil. The pressure was intense as his mind searched for meaningful subject material.

Paul's thoughts frantically raced as he thought about the mysterious old man. *Had Barnaby, through osmosis, transferred a topic into his brain that would eventually enlighten him? Was he under some sort of hypnotic spell that would soon reveal itself? Would a paranormal event occur which would seize him and magically direct him to produce a literary masterpiece?* Nonsense, he reasoned, but it sure would be nice.

More questions popped up as he recalled past events with the old man. *Had any of the visits held a clue? Was he to relate biographical successes of any of the people which Barnaby had referred? Did the silver penny signify that he was supposed to talk about economics? Perhaps, as he remembered the ants, he should speak about ecology. Or, were the grains of sand compared to the stars in the universe his cue to talk about the world and man's relationship to it.* Nothing seemed right.

Suddenly, there was a faint knock at the front door. Paul grabbed his glass, finished his pop and went to answer the door.

It was Timothy. "Hi, Paul."

"Hey, Tim, what's going on?"

"I was with Barnaby at the park earlier today and he wanted me to give this to you." Timothy reached into his right front trouser pocket and revealed a folded, sealed business sized envelope.

Paul accepted the letter. "How did you know where I lived? Hey, where's Silas? Is Barnaby still at Sunny View?"

Timothy started laughing by being asked so many questions. "Uh, Barnaby told me where you lived . . . see, I told you he knew everything. Let me think. Silas is still at the park watching squirrels and chipmunks. I'm pretty sure The Captain left because he said he had some business to attend to."

Paul looked over Timothy's head and up at the sky. Giant cumulonimbus clouds were forming overhead. Their ominous presence indicated to Paul a thunderstorm may be developing soon.

"C'mon in, Timothy. It looks like it might rain. Plus, we can open this envelope and see what Barnaby told you to give me."

Paul pointed Timothy to his bedroom. "Hey, do you want something to drink?"

"Yeah, anything. It's hot and muggy outside. This air conditioning feels good!" Timothy walked himself to Paul's room and sat in the chair.

Retrieving the two liter bottle of soda, Paul grabbed an extra glass for Timothy as he, too, went back to his bedroom. Setting the tumblers on his desk, he poured pop into each as he tried to eyeball equal amounts. "There's not much left," Paul remarked. "We only get a half empty glass."

"That's okay," Timothy replied. "Anyway, it looks half full to me."

"That's what I just said," Paul sarcastically corrected.

Timothy smirked, "Sort of, but not really." He then sipped his soda. "Oh, well, open the letter."

Paul held the envelope to the light of the window to see the silhouette of its contents. Pinching one end of it, he shook it as the paper inside slid to one end. Carefully, he tore open the opposite end. Bowing the envelope, he shook the note out into his other hand. He opened the folded message and began to read.

"Number one. 'Change your thoughts and your change your world.' Norman Vincent Peale. Number two. 'Always seek out the seed of triumph in every adversity.' Og Mandino. Number three. 'Optimism is the faith that leads to achievement. Nothing can be done without hope and confidence.' Helen Keller. And, the last one, number four. 'One's positive thoughts insure many ideal satisfying moments.' Barnaby."

"Wow. What's all that supposed to mean?" Timothy questioned.

Paul then related his story about the speech he had to present at the school's graduation ceremonies. "I guess Barnaby is trying to motivate me. He knew I wasn't happy that I had to compose a speech. I asked him for help. But, he said I must do it on my own. It's like when your parents tell you to do something because it's supposed to be good for you."

"Yeah, it doesn't sound much like you want to do it," Timothy agreed. "But remember, Barnaby's always right. Maybe you should read those notes, again. Maybe if you change your thoughts, you'll change your mind. Barnaby once told me if you change your thoughts, you change your life. It's like thinking nice things rather than worrying all the time."

"Sounds like the old man," Paul muttered. He looked down at the letter and began reading, again.

Meanwhile, Timothy looked at a shelf above Paul's desk where some books were resting. Although somewhat tattered, he recognized one of the titles. The book, *The Wizard of Oz*, was nudged between two other volumes.

"Hey, neat!" Timothy exclaimed. "I've got that book, too. It's cool how Dorothy, the Scarecrow, Tin Man and Cowardly Lion all go to Oz to see the Wizard for something they each want. They're happy a lot, too . . . singing about following the yellow brick road and stuff."

"Right," Paul uttered "Even though the Wicked Witch of the West was always trying to make it rough for them, they stuck it out."

"Yeah," Timothy nodded his head in agreement. "Having faith and hoping they'd get their stuff."

"Yup," Paul replied, halfheartedly listening while he read, adding, "they were pretty confident."

As if on cue, Timothy turned to look at Paul as Paul looked at Tim. "Optimism!" they chimed together.

At that moment, a loud clap of thunder shook the house. Timothy's eyes widened as a startled Paul nervously forced a grin. Paul jumped to look out the window. The rain storm he suspected had quickly arrived. Flashes of lightning flared in the sky. Blinding electrical bolts pierced the looming grey clouds. Towards the horizon, an eerie shade of yellow blanketed the sky as the sun tried to cast its rays. The rain pelted the roof of the house like the nonstop bulleting of rifle fire.

Gaining his composure, Timothy wiggled out of his chair and followed Paul to the window. "That was pretty spooky, Paul."

Paul continued watching the rain. Just as quickly as it spastically developed, it had now resigned to a calm, steady downpour. "Yeah, pretty weird. It was as if Barnaby planned what was going to happen."

Timothy shook his head in disbelief. "I told ya', Paul, Barnaby . . ."

"I know, I know. You already told me. Barnaby knows everything!" Paul exasperated.

Paul returned to the side of his desk. He continued to study the note Timothy had delivered to him. Of particular importance now was what Barnaby had expressed. He slightly mumbled the words to himself again,

"One's positive thoughts insure many ideal satisfying moments. "Tim," he called. "Take a look at this closer. There's something funny about this that I can't figure out. See if you can. I can't concentrate."

Timothy took the letter from Paul. He sat back down and spread out the note as he pressed its edges firmly on the table. Then, word by word, he slowly repeated the sentence as his right forefinger delicately hovered over every letter, "one's . . . pos . . . i . . . tive . . . thoughts . . . in . . . sure . . . ma . . . ny . . . i . . . de . . . al . . . sa . . . tis . . . fy . . . ing . . . mo . . . ments." He repeated it again a little more quickly, "One's   . . .   positive . . . thoughts . . . insure . . . many . . . ideal . . . satisfying . . . moments. As Paul impatiently folded his arms across his chest and being disturbed, started tapping his foot, Timothy fluently recited it a third time, "One's positive thoughts insure many ideal satisfying moments. I think I've got it!" he exclaimed.

"Got what? What did you come up with?" Paul anxiously asked.

"It's an acronym, Paul," Timothy confidently assured. "Take the first letter of each word in the sentence and it spells optimism. The sentence defines the word!"

"Let me see," Paul urged as he picked up the paper and examined it more closely.

"I'll bet Barnaby wanted us to figure that out," guessed Timothy. "He knows I like games like that. Remember what I told you about Silas' name?"

Paul had no choice but to agree with his friend. "I guess you're right, Tim."

"So, is it helping any?" Timothy asked Paul. "Do you feel better about giving your speech, now?"

"Let me think a minute," Paul answered as he took a drink of his soda.

Timothy reached up for *The Wizard of Oz* and started paging through it, rekindling memories of the memorable fantasy. Paul reflectively returned his gaze out his bedroom window as the rain became less severe. He was trying to correlate how optimism related to different subjects that he and the old man talked about.

First, he recounted how Barnaby initially startled him and how the conversation about 'attitude' ensued. Obviously, optimism was a determinant about attitude. The concept seemed so simple, now. To be more positive about everyday situations and their outcomes would certainly reduce stress levels. He even recalled reading in the news lately that less stress is better for a person's overall health. Then, he remembered him and Barnaby talking about 'integrity.' This idea was also easy to understand. When someone maintains high morals in their thinking, their optimism would increase because they know they are doing what is right. Next, he thought about 'perseverance.' Always striving for successful completion in given endeavors defined this, so optimism was certainly a factor. 'Never give up,' he thought, as he faintly remembered the quote from the Winston Churchill history lesson. He looked at Timothy, still rummaging through the pages and recollected their day at the playground. Barnaby had implanted many insightful speculations that Easter Sunday. Basically, he reasoned, the activities Timothy had engaged in that day were performances by virtue of moral excellence. That was absolutely optimistic. Finally, he fondly recalled his most recent meeting with the old man. Looking out the window at a tree, he saw new growths of leaves glistening from the moisture the rain had deposited on them. Their glimmering reminded him of 'reflection' which summed up that day's discussions. Yes, reflecting on one's mettle and trying to improve was certainly an optimistic action. Paul's eyes softened as he managed a slight grin to himself. He marveled at the old man's genius. The manner in which he crocheted colorful yarns of character into an afghan of spirit and determination was amazing.

Timothy, satisfied with his review of the book, finished his refreshment and looked up at Paul. "Are you finished thinking, now?"

"Yes, I believe I am," Paul confidently responded.

"Okay, so what are you going to talk about?" Timothy pressed.

"Well, I'm not quite sure, yet. But, I'm . . . optimistic," he smiled.

"The Captain steered you right, eh?" Timothy smirked.

"Yes," Paul nodded resolutely, "he is quite a navigator."

"Aye, aye," Timothy saluted. "But, I better get going. The rain looks like it has almost stopped and my parents might be worried about me."

"Good idea," Paul agreed.

They both finished their sodas and Paul led Timothy to the front door. Bidding farewell, Timothy descended the front porch steps, skipped to the sidewalk, and started jogging home. Paul watched. The rain sprinkled lightly now. The sun coaxed the clouds to move on and the damp ground was quickly drying. Paul stepped out onto the porch. Inhaling deeply, he absorbed the fresh clean air so reminiscent following a sudden thunderstorm. He looked towards the sky. In the distance was a magnificent striking rainbow. He dreamed about what was beyond it . . . just like Dorothy in *The Wizard of Oz*.

PREPARATION

The second Sunday of May found Paul restlessly lying in his bed into the late morning. He was still trying to contain his optimism from the previous week. He was energized and ready to tackle his assignment once and for all. He was anxious to get this monkey off his back. Now, he only had to focus on the subject matter for his speech. Perhaps a visit to the Lincoln Library would offer a clue.

Paul felt guilty as he walked to the library. He could not recall the last time he had been there. He did remember, however, when he was younger and his father took him. The library had a program that encouraged reading. Every time Paul read a book, he would get a ticket punched. After a certain number of punches, Paul was rewarded with a prize at a local business. He reasoned that this, along with his parents reading to him when he was a child, instilled the positive values of reading good books.

Upon entering the library, Paul was greeted with a much different environment than when he was last there. He saw multiple workstations of computers with people of all ages occupying them. Nearby, the newest arrivals of fiction and non-fiction works were prominently displayed. Shiny slanted metal book shelves housed the most current periodicals as local newspapers were spread along its base. Roaming the floor, Paul saw a large selection of compact discs. Various artists from a wide variety of musical interests were available for listeners to borrow. A free standing unit housed a large variety of books on CDs. Movies were also available to rent for free. He scanned the titles, recognizing many of the current names.

Paul continued his investigation. From his vantage point, he could now observe a 360 degree view of the entire library and its arrangement. Behind him was the front counter where librarians and volunteers assisted patrons. To his left, the children's section dominated the area. Paul felt this planning was excellent. It was located close to the front desk which could provide help to the toddlers who may need it. Also, it was designed with an open and inviting area to encourage young readers to visit.

Smaller tables and chairs enticed children to sit and enjoy their stay. Straight ahead were countless volumes arranged by the author's names. Paul recognized this as being the area for fiction books. Teens as well as adults were strolling the aisles trying to locate their favorite essayist or the title of a manuscript that was of interest to them. Lastly, Paul peered to his right. This is where he thought he may find the information he needed. It was home to The Dewey Decimal Classification System.

Paul was somewhat familiar with The Dewey Decimal System. The main thing he knew was that most of its non-fiction works were classified by subject matter. He reasoned, as he searched the different topic contents, an idea would emerge and he could formulate an informative speech. Signs posted on the ends of the book shelves assisted him. This information divided aisles of books into ten subject areas and again into ten subdivisions. By reading the classification numbers, Paul was able to determine the subject matter it contained.

Paul walked to the beginning of the systemized collection. Here, he found books that provided 'General Works,' or information. He immediately thought of the old man. It seemed to Paul that Barnaby was somewhat of an encyclopedia himself. He quickly scanned this small section, occasionally choosing a title for a brief review. Satisfied, Paul reached into his back pocket and retrieved his folded notebook paper and pen. Unfolding it and firmly pressing it against his thigh, he scrolled the word 'information.'

The 'Philosophy and Psychology' section blended into the next array of books. Deeming this most appropriate for his quest, Paul's thoughts remained centered on the old man. Clustered together were a variety of books attributed to a positive mental attitude. Walking his fingers meticulously across the binders, Paul whispered the titles. When one stimulated his interest, he carefully removed it from its location and scanned the back jacket. He would then turn to the chapters at the beginning of the book. If one was particularly captivating, he would leaf through the pages and absorb the ideas of the author. In fact, he recognized the names of a few of these writers as ones which Barnaby referred. Paul spent a considerable amount of time browsing these books. They provided rich insight as Paul penned the word 'positive.'

Appropriately, the 'Religion' classification followed. This assembly of works included a variety of subjects reflecting different theological viewpoints and how they related to various circumstances, situations, and conditions. Paul stretched his perspective. He gained comfort in the fact that in the United States of America, the First Amendment in The Bill of Rights to the U. S. Constitution guarantees the freedom to exercise personal religious beliefs. He added the word 'inspiration' to his list.

Man's place in the world and his interactions are how Paul summarized the abundant 'Social Sciences' division. The many volumes included subjects pertaining to interpersonal relationships, economics, finance and law. Paul did not have any experience in these matters, but made a mental note of the significant attention dedicated to this discipline. He hastened onward as he jotted down the word 'communication.'

Next was an area Paul speculated he would enjoy. It was labeled 'Language.' Basically, it involved communication. Paul enjoyed the magic of the alphabet. He was an aficionado of crossword puzzles and word searches. It did not hurt, either, that he prided himself in spelling. Synonyms, antonyms, and homonyms were especially easy for him to understand. As if a predetermined patron in a perfectly prose panacea, alliteration and assonance gripped him. Consonance also seized his fascination. Paul dabbled in rhyming, and like a game, challenged his mind to parody literary and musical works. Time flew by as he studied countless tomes. In precise penmanship he penned 'rhetoric.'

'Natural Sciences and Mathematics' identified the sixth section. This, again, reminded him of the old man as he gazed at the titles highlighting astronomy, insects, and plant life. He recalled how Barnaby patiently lectured him about the stars, ants, and trees. He sensed this was an 'analogy' as he good naturedly printed the word next to the number six.

As Paul left the Natural Sciences, he embarked upon books about 'Technology.' Paul always wished he could invent something, but figured he was just not wired intellectually enough to create something involved with applied science. He did respect the individuals who were so gifted. Their improvements upon devices continually elevated the progress of man. He saw this area as 'limitless.'

Paul forayed into 'The Arts.' Structure, architecture, and design dominated his thinking. Contentment solaced him as he reminisced entering Sunny View Park. 'The Professor' weaved his way into Paul's mind. The profound teacher belonged on one of these shelves. Everyone should have the opportunity to witness such a statue. He imagined what theory 'The Professor' would propose. Whatever, Paul reassured, it would be as solid as the pedestal base that supported his granite friend. Smiling to himself as if mentally connected to his stoic teacher, Paul inscribed the word 'nobility'.

Shuffling on, Paul embarked upon 'Literature.' This seemed a dichotomy to him. As much as he loved to dissect, analyze and interpret the English language, Paul found it difficult to discern great literary works. He did, however, have a dream. It was a goal which he expressed to no one. He imagined someday he would publish a manuscript that would possess literary value. Perhaps his creation would have a positive influence. Maybe the way he . . . arranged letters of the alphabet . . . into words of various lengths . . . resulting in powerfully placed sentences of a paragraph . . . molded into a mighty manuscript . . . which would enlighten just one mind. That would be reward enough. He stared at his piece of paper and contemplated. 'Personal' is what flowed from his pen.

'Geography and History' completed the ten classifications of The Dewey Decimal System. Once again, his thoughts focused on Barnaby. He even pictured the old man next to him reaching for selected items to forage through. What, he wondered, would be the next tidbit of information that he would learn from the old man? Nearing the bottom of his list, Paul etched 'education'.

Paul continued past the history section and was greeted by many volumes of biographies, an endless supply it seemed, of people who dared to make a difference. He admired their drive, determination, desire, dedication and discipline. These were distinct qualities that separated focused men and women, who stood high and above others, from those who only settled for mediocrity.

Paul had lost all track of time. It was close to 5:00 p.m. and the library was to close soon. Surely, he thought, he would have made more progress on his speech. All he had were ten words listed on a piece of paper that he wrote for seemingly no known reason. Refolding the paper, he returned it to his back pocket. He gave one final look at the rows of books in the aisle and proceeded to the front door.

As Paul approached the exit, his eyes glanced over to a sign. It resembled a calendar but contained different information. It was a poster that identified different facts about the month of May. It listed the different observances various societies and organizations paid special attention to during the month. Additionally, weekly appreciations and daily monitoring were also highlighted.

Pausing, Paul stepped closer to the placard. Engraved across the top in bold black letters read 'MAY IS GET CAUGHT READING MONTH.' How appropriate, Paul mused, as it had certainly caught his attention. His eyes lowered as he continued skimming. 'OLDER AMERICAN'S MONTH' and 'TEEN SELF-ESTEEM MONTH' were also included in the list. Maybe this information, Paul wondered, would be helpful. Not wanting to take any chances on remembering, he quickly removed the paper from his pocket and scribbled the phrases on the back.

With only a couple minutes left, Paul scanned the remaining data. He saw within the first weeks of May, 'TEACHER APPRECIATION WEEK' had come and gone. 'READING IS FUN WEEK' and 'FRIENDS WEEK' were also indicated as arriving soon. Paul felt these three phrases were somehow interconnected and also scratched more notes. The obvious yearly holiday highlighted was 'MEMORIAL DAY' and it was being observed on Monday, May twenty-fifth. Paul's and the rest of the senior class' last day was Friday, May twenty-second. That evening was the due date of his assignment.

When Paul arrived home he was disturbed by mixed emotions. He was certain that by going to the library his speech would be nearing completion. Instead, however, it was only nearing the beginning. Heading straight to his bedroom, he was unsure if he would try to conjure material for the sake of productivity; or, should he risk everything and rely on the weekend before the due date and orchestrate a symphony of dictation. Paul laughed at himself. He knew he was no conductor. His hope was to fall somewhere in between.

Sitting at his desk, Paul retrieved the note paper from his pocket and set it on the table. He read the list of words he had written on the one side. Flipping it over, he studied the phrases. One more time, Paul turned it over and looked at the words. Perhaps if he rewrote these on a separate piece of paper it would spark creativity. After all, a speech would need notes and this was as good as any place to begin.

Paul slowly printed the ten words one below the other. He allowed a lined space between each one. This, he reasoned, would not clutter his thoughts as he tried to find a connection. He contemplated the phrases, but still nothing materialized. So, reaching in his desk drawer for scissors, Paul cut out each individual word. Then, he placed them next to each other as if they already were a sentence. In order, the words . . . 'information, positive, inspiration, communication, rhetoric, analogy, limitless, nobility, personal, and education' stared back at Paul. Again, he reviewed the May monthly observances statements. 'OLDER AMERICAN' and 'TEEN' boldly shouted back, making him think of Barnaby and Timothy. What if he did some rearrangement? So, sliding some of the words around, he created a different order. Nothing. He tried again but to no avail. Not one to give up so quickly, Paul kept working at it. Finally, after what seemed like an hour of frustration, Paul formed a rudimentary order . . . 'education . . . analogy . . . positive . . . inspiration . . . rhetoric . . . communication . . . limitless . . . information . . . personal . . . nobility.' After adding grammatical variations, Paul scribbled . . . 'educational analogy,' . . . 'positive inspirational rhetoric,' . . . 'communicates limitless information,' . . . and 'personal nobility.' As if someone were guiding his hand, he then developed a phrase which stated, 'Educational analogies of positive inspirational rhetoric that communicates limitless information for personal nobility.' Paul's curiosity was aroused. He grinned as his thoughts once again returned to the old man. This was exactly what Barnaby strived for in Paul these past weeks.

Not to be satisfied, Paul believed there was more. He firmly believed it pertained to Timothy because of the manner in which the word 'TEEN' nagged at him. After copying the mystically originated quote on a brand new sheet of filler paper, Paul once more began sliding the clipped letters in various positions to create a sentence. It was as if he was operating a literary Ouija Board. Then, after requiring more time than his initial solution, he again settled on an order for no known reason. It read . . . analogy . . . positive . . . rhetoric . . . inspiration . . . nobility . . . communication . . . information . . . personal . . . limitless . . . education. This time, he just stared at the words as they appeared in succession. The letters blearily pulsated. Some lost their focus. Paul thought of the time he asked Timothy for help with Barnaby's quote. Then, as if by revelation, he wrote down the first letters of each word. A. P. R. I. N. C. I. P. L. E. Now, it was obvious. Hidden in the formation was a clue. A PRINCIPLE. It was a doctrine that was meant to teach. Barnaby's influence was being bestowed upon Paul, using Timothy as an instrument.

Paul's mind raced uncontrollably. He thought of Barnaby, Timothy and 'The Professor.' He recalled the names of famous people the old man had mentioned during their reflective discussions. He remembered how challenging events make us mightier if we allow them. He reminisced the way the old man conveyed his messages using anything from a simple object to abstract ideas. He reflected on how much he had grown since he first met his mentor. At first his vision was skewed. A dense fog seemed to lift from his vision and he could now see more clearly. Everything was in focus.

Paul had one more loose end to tie before he began preparing his speech. He hoped that what he needed was where he saw it last. He made his way to the basement and turned on the light. Across the room, a small library of books his family had accumulated over the years lined the wall. Paul approached the shelves. Running his hand across the bindings, he searched for the one with the worn yellow jacket that his father had used as a daily devotional for inspiration. Nestled between a book about Lincoln, and one authored by Mandino, rested the prized volume. Paul gracefully inched it from its domain, brushed away the light dust, and cradled it in his arm. Deftly, he thumbed through the pages. Satisfaction flashed across his face. He slapped the book shut and raced with it upstairs to his bedroom. Now, he would begin his assignment. It was as if the final precious piece of a prized puzzle had precariously fallen into perfect place.

INSTRUCTION

Graduation finally arrived. Paul stood on the stage of the gymnasium and looked across to the twelve empty evenly spaced chairs. This is where the seniors would sit. A podium dissected the row so there were six on either side. Since Paul was to be the speaker, he had no need to have a place, but did set a chair aside for himself, if needed. He felt proud as he read a banner that was strung across as a backdrop. It serendipitously read . . . 'Yesterday's Dreams Determine Today's Actions for Tomorrow's Achievements.' This effectively evoked what Paul was to speak about.

He then surveyed the arena as people slowly filtered in. The setup was just as Paul had envisioned. Eight rows of folding chairs were reserved at the front for the middle and high school students. Sixth graders occupied the seats closest to the front as ascending grades chose seats closer to the back. Then, two rows were assigned for faculty, staff, and administrators. The rest of the gym was available for friends, family, and relatives. Paul smiled to himself. How lucky, he felt, to be part of such a small close-knit community. A tinge of nostalgia settled upon him. He then joined his twelve other classmates in the hallway as the evening's program was about to begin.

At precisely 7:00 p.m., Principal Sain approached the podium. Collecting his thoughts, he waited as muffled conversations and the stirring and shuffling of attendees subsided. Then, he welcomed the audience and proceeded with the usual fare. First, he thanked everyone. Secondly, he recapped the school year. He summarized the school's academic achievements, its role in the community, and the School Board's vision for the future. He spoke of the extracurricular activities as he promoted the sports and academic programs. Lastly, trying to keep it brief, it was his responsibility to honor the Senior class with their diplomas and any Certificates of Recognition. This would, in turn, lead into Paul's presentation.

Principal Sain alphabetically called each graduate individually from the hallway. One by one, they emerged as they heard their name. Applause was bestowed upon them as they made their way to the podium. After a

71

quick handshake and congratulatory remark, they received their diploma. They then found their way to their assigned seats. Paul, the last to enter, remained standing next to Principal Sain.

"Tonight," Mr. Sain began, "we have an unprecedented event. At midterm, I asked Paul if he would share some departing wisdom with us as this Senior class embarks upon a new journey that we know as 'life.' Ever agreeable, he welcomed the opportunity to share his thoughts. So, without further ado, let us thank Paul for his insight and reflection, as I know we are eager to hear what he has to say."

Paul, swallowing the smoothed over introduction, smiled and nodded to the audience. Then, he reached into his suit coat pocket for a small stack of recipe sized note cards.

"Thank you, Mr. Sain," Paul began. "I appreciate the opportunity to address everybody in attendance. I hope what I have to say somehow finds its way into everyone's heart and embeds itself into their soul. If at any time in the future, you recall what I have said and it made you feel better about yourself, I believe I have successfully completed this assignment."

"Before I continue, though," Paul said, "I would like to tell you that May is a pretty special month." His eyes then shifted to where Mr. Sain had taken his seat. "May first was Principal's Day and I would just like to take this moment to honor our school's administration team. Congratulations. Please stand." Paul initiated clapping as everyone joined in. Then, as his eyes swept the middle of the gymnasium where the instructors were sitting, he added, "I would also like to thank all of the teachers. Many of you are probably unaware that from May third through May ninth of this month was 'Teacher Appreciation Week' with May the fifth being 'National Teacher's Day.' Educators, may you stand now, please." Again, Paul led the applause as a common look of bewilderment was evidenced across the many faces of Paul's mentors.

"Finally, in keeping with the spirit of education and instruction, I would like to honor librarians everywhere as last week was 'Reading is Fun Week.' Many times we take this special gift for granted. A whole new world to investigate awaits an individual when he opens a motivating book. The journey he travels can take him to destinations he never would have dreamed about. It happened to me. I have been on a journey of self-discovery for the past three months, but only within the past week have I been able to synthesize what I have discovered by paging through a book. Tonight, I would like to share that with you."

Scanning the first page of his note cards, Paul began his oration. "First, I would like to start by saying that many different things happen in an individual's life. Some are good, and some are not so good. The good events are fun, rewarding, and make us happy. The bad however, are painful, punishing, and filled with sadness. The good, which often escapes memory because of the sweet swiftness of which they pass, coax us to perform at our best - being at the top of our game. While the bad, seeming to loom forever, foretell grief, discouragement and disappointment. These external episodes, in effect, determine our attitude. Surely, positive conditions need no adjustments. However, I am here today to convince you that unfortunate circumstances need not be looked at negatively.

"Our attitude is actually a choice. When we confront an event over which we have no control, we must not let it dictate our disposition. Yes, we can feel our emotions. But, we must not dispense ill will towards ourselves or others. It is imperative we remain in control and channel our energy into maintaining an enthusiastic demeanor. This wisdom will engage a positive spirit and assist us in overcoming unpleasant situations. No, it is not easy. However, we must realize the resistance to something of which we have no power to change is only wasted energy. When we choose to stay upbeat we make a decision to prevail. That . . . is having a positive attitude.

"As we adopt a positive attitude we open doors for ourselves. People see us in a brighter light. We no longer harbor a 'doom and gloom' existence and are actually more pleasant to be around. We give more of ourselves and get more in return from others. Respect grows. Character develops. Praise is given and received. Appreciation and gratitude are nurtured. A truly mature individual is born. Let me repeat myself, we choose our attitudes.

"Next, I would like to segue to integrity. We must govern ourselves and commit to a strict adherence of incorruptible morals and values. As in our attitudes, it begins with our thought process. As I have learned, thoughts are things. We must be aware of how we think. Because, our thoughts soon become our words; our words dictate our actions; our actions becomes habit; habit defines our character; and, our character determines our destiny. Yes, we must watch how we think according to Lao Tzu.

"How do we do this? We must be credible. The only way to we elevate ourselves to this level is by being truthful and honest with ourselves. We cannot fool our subconscious mind. Being self-obedient develops posture. When others see our principled, dignified actions, it reveals traits of reliability and dependability. Our stature is fashioned. Is it difficult? Definitely. Is it achievable? Definitely. How? By the third process . . . perseverance. Now, 'Ds' are not very good on a report card; but, the following 'Ds' are worthy to incorporate into our psyche. Number one is to be dedicated. One must not let his thoughts waver from a worthy cause. Next, determination allows an individual to focus on his goal. Following that, he must develop a drive to succeed. He has to be diligent - nothing must obstruct his path. Overall, he has to possess a desire to be disciplined. There may be times when we encounter resistance. When these arise, we need to tolerate the adverse circumstances, call upon our inner strength, and be tenacious enough to forge ahead. Our consistent persistence will pay us great dividends.

"Finally, how do we do this? Optimistically! When we have a belief in ourselves it instills confidence. Aspirations evolve and we become inspired. This breeds happiness and positive motivation. Creativity blossoms and expectant patience dominates. Faith and hope tag team for the fruition of desires. This, in turn, completes the circle by having the free will to choose. I know I will be taking these disciplines - a positive attitude, Lincolnesque integrity, extraordinary perseverance, and eternal optimism - with me as I embark upon the next chapter of my life. I hope you will too. Thank you."

Paul wanted to continue, but a thunderous applause erupted. Slowly, interspersed individuals rose to their feet. Soon, the entire gymnasium was standing, clapping, and smiling. His father wore an ear-to-ear grin as his mother's eyes blurred with tears. Mr. Sain held his hands high as his cupped hands sliced the air above him. The rambunctious front rows of sixth and seventh graders pounded their fists in the air, swinging at imaginary punching bags.

Paul raised his arm in the air, forefinger pointing to the ceiling as he tried to subdue the appreciative crowd. Smiling, he added, "Now, there is one more weekly observance that is happening this month that I would like to recognize." The audience hushed as he rearranged his note cards. "Earlier, I spoke about some daily and weekly observances that occur in the month of May. Well, we happen to be at the end of the week known as 'National Old and New Friends Week.'" He then looked to his right and left where the rest of the senior class was seated. Grinning, he added, "So,

I can think of no better way to honor my classmates, my friends - than to allow them to participate in the closing of this convocation."

Surprised, the students apprehensively exchanged looks with each other as their eyes settled back upon Paul. Raising his other hand in the air, Paul showed everyone the note cards. "I have written something on each one of these twelve cards. I am going to pass them out to my classmates. Individually, I would like them to read what it says, and, if they so choose, to summarize their thoughts of the message. In the spirit of this evening's festivities, I am confident you will enjoy it."

Paul then walked to one end of the row of students. One by one, he handed out a card as he passed in front of each person. When he delivered the last one, he stepped aside the row and directed the group.

"First of all, we have Suzette. Please stand and read what is printed on your card," Paul directed.

Nervously, the petite blond haired, blue eyed girl rose and stood at her chair as a deafening silence filled the auditorium. She began, "Parents can only give good advice or put them on the right paths, but the final forming of a person's character lies in their own hands." Ooohs and aahs echoed in the room as appreciative grins reflected on many of the fathers' and mothers' faces. "This was spoken by Anne Frank," Suzette continued. "I remember learning about her in history class. She was a Jewish girl who was imprisoned in a concentration camp and wrote a famous diary about her experiences. I believe she was fifteen years old when she died. I think what it means is that parents really try to teach us to be the best that we can. But, after we graduate and we're on our own, we are responsible to ourselves to be the best that we can be. Thank you." Suzette then smiled, bowed slightly while nodding her head, and obediently sat down.

Before the audience could break into applause, Paul quickly stepped up to the podium. "That was great, Suzette. Just as we planned, right?" The crowd broke into a chuckle as Paul continued. "I think my classmates are going to offer more great ideals. Let's please refrain from clapping after each reading and show our appreciation at the end of the presentation. Thank you." Paul then introduced Anthony.

As Anthony rose, he steadied his card between his thumbs and forefingers and read, "The greater danger for most of us lies not in setting our aim too high and falling short; but in setting our aim too low, and achieving our mark." Anthony looked up at the audience. "Even though Michelangelo was best known for his paintings and sculptures, I believe

75

what this means is that he wanted people to always try to do and be their best. We have to ask ourselves that when we reach a goal that we set for ourselves, could we have done more by trying a little harder and doing a little more? We shouldn't be content with mediocrity. Let's strive for excellence. We may surprise ourselves at our accomplishments." As Anthony sat down he thought about how appropriate that particular card was for him because he had earned a scholarship to study art in college.

Paul stood up. "Great job! Next, we have Jaclynne. Go ahead."

Jaclynne studied her card as Paul sat down. When she was ready, she stood and took three steps toward the front of the stage. Looking up, she paused and demanded their attention, "'Do not go where the path may lead; go instead where there is no path and leave a trail' . . . Ralph Waldo Emerson." Confidently, she stated her interpretation. "Mr. Emerson, poet and philosopher, would want us to strive to become leaders. As we grow, we must believe in our convictions and go forth with our own decisions and choices. We do not always have to do what others think we must. As long as our moral compass is pointed in a true direction and we are not sidelined with corrupt thoughts, we can become effective teachers." Jaclynne stared straight ahead, again, pausing for effect. She then scanned the crowd from left to right and front to back. Without turning around, she backed up the three steps and took her seat. Folding her hands in her lap, she remained stoically staring straight ahead as Paul prepared to introduce the next student.

Joshua, however, was ahead of the game. Self-declared class clown, he had already stood up and was grinning from ear to ear.

"Joshua," Paul commented, "it appears you're ready. What can you tell us?"

Joshua had spent the previous moments memorizing his instructed advice. With forethought effect, he opened his arms to the audience and palms facing outward as if posing a question, he asked, "The difference between school and life? In school, you're taught a lesson and then given a test. In life, you're given a test that teaches you a lesson." Perfectly delivered, he smiled as he rigidly placed his left arm across his stomach. His right arm did the same behind his back. He bowed, straightened up and saluted as he energetically expressed the 'm' sound on the name, "Tom Bodett." Then, posing a second question, he sarcastically ad-libbed, "More tests? I thought school was over!" Fully satisfied, he smiled again as he clicked his heels, nodded, and sat back down.

Paul meekly smiled as he slightly shook his head from side to side. He silently figured that Joshua's animation was delivered at just the right time as a stress reliever to the night's activities and who better than Joshua to accomplish this?

Phyllis patiently waited for her cue from Paul to take her turn. When Paul did, she quickly and obediently stood. Glancing at her card for reassurance, Phyllis succinctly orated, "Mine has to do with college as we leave our high school years . . . "If you think education is expensive, try ignorance." I am not sure who he was, but it was stated by Derek Bok." Phyllis then systematically sat back down.

The pace of the presentations seemed to increase. It was now Barrett's turn as he compliantly rose and read, "A teacher affects eternity; he can never tell where his influence stops." It says here that it was spoken by Henry B. Adams. Thank you." Barrett then sat back down.

Many of the parents' heads nodded and focused towards the teachers as the instructors' faces revealed smiles of appreciation. Paul then decided to interject a few comments of his own. "For those of you who are unsure of the identities of the owners' of the latest quotes, I can be of assistance since I was the one who did the research on them. I think many of us can identify with Tom Bodett and his famous line on that television commercial. Anyway, as for Derek Bok and Henry B. Adams," as Paul slyly grinned, "let me just say they have Harvard University in common and that everyone in attendance can learn more valuable things about them if they do a little investigating themselves. You're never too old to learn" As a few chuckles and groans echoed the room, Paul continued, "Okay, Therese, you're up."

"We have another quotation about teachers," Therese announced, "and it is an old Chinese proverb. Teachers open the door, but you must enter by yourself. This is almost like what Paul just got finished saying. It simply means that a teacher can ignite a spark in us, whatever it may be but it is up to us to fan the flame and keep the fire in us burning. We must do things for ourselves. When we do that, we instill confidence in our abilities to achieve our goals."

"Very good, Therese," Paul complimented. "Mat, your turn."

Mat, well-liked and philosophic, seemed to relish the card that was chosen for him. He remained seated, lifted his legs, and crossed them in his chair. He then brought his palms together, thumbs resting against his chest, and pointed his fingers to the air as if in a praying position.

"Additional wisdom attributed to the Far East and Theosophy," he drably recited. Then, glancing downward, he proclaimed, "When the student is ready, teacher will appear." Looking up, he peered over the heads of the audience staring at no one in particular. A respectful hush fell over the crowd. "Perfect," Paul added, smiling at the emotional variety and successful direction his unrehearsed creative idea was taking. "It seems everyone is identifying perfectly with their assigned cards. Let's proceed. Janette, you're next."

Wanting to get her turn over as quickly as possible, Janette abruptly rose and delved into her selection without delay. "Here is another saying by Ralph Waldo Emerson, who, by the way, was a good friend of Henry David Thoreau, "'Life is a succession of lessons, which must be lived to be understood.'" I think this is like the saying 'experience is the best teacher.'"

Janette sat down and nudged DeWayne. "Your turn," she whispered as Paul nodded in approval.

DeWayne, rereading his passage for the third time, stood up slowly and looked out to the audience. "This one is kind of long so you have to pay attention." He began, "'In the case of good books, the point is not how many of them you can get through, but rather how many can get through to you.'" This was by Mortimer J. Adler."

DeWayne quizzically looked to where Paul was standing. Paul sensed he did not realize who Adler was, so he smoothly assisted him. "Mortimer Adler, for those of you who do not know, was an American author and educator." Relieved at his rescue, DeWayne nervously smiled and carefully sat back down as Paul motioned to Jocelyn to continue.

The appropriateness of this quotation to Jocelyn made her feel special. Internally driven and competitively motivated, she recalled her athletic victories as she stood and emphatically stated, "I've worked too hard and too long to let anything stand in the way of my goals. I will not let my teammates down and I will not let myself down." Jocelyn continued, "Mia Hamm, who was a famous female soccer player, said that. I believe it says three important things. First, it tells of personal ambition. Secondly, it includes individuals working together as a team like we are doing now. And third, it states the importance of a person striving to achieve her goals. Thank you," she added, and dutifully sat down.

"Excellent," Paul inspired. "Julian, last but not least, let's hear what you have to say."

Julian gave a slightly embarrassed grin to the crowd as he stood up, waved his right hand, and began, "'It is a good thing for an uneducated man to read books of quotations,' by Winston Churchill." Julian reflectively placed his forefinger under his chin and summarized, "I believe that words can be very powerful motivators, as evidenced here tonight. I am going to try to remember a lot of what was said and who said it. In fact, it makes me curious to try to find out more positive quotations by many other people. Thank you."

As Julian sat down, Paul returned to the podium. "Ladies and gentlemen, I also have one that was spoken by Epictetus, a Greek sage who lived around 100 A.D." Pausing for effect, Paul softly and directly spoke, "If you wish to be a writer, write." Again he paused for effect. Then, he gave his interpretation. "Of course, this means if you want to be an author then write books. But, it also means if you want to be an artist, then paint pictures; if you want to build houses, then be a carpenter; if you want to help people, then be a doctor. Basically, it means you can be anything that you want to be. Do not let anyone steal your dream from you. Follow your heart. Focus on your goal and incorporate all of your energy to its completion. Overcome any setbacks by persevering and realize success is in the journey, not the destination. Spread these words to others as you embark upon your careers. Thank you."

The crowd stood and applauded as Paul returned to the side of the stage. He then turned to his fellow students and motioned for them to stand. As they did, the din persisted. Paul clapped for his classmates and they clapped for him. The senior class bowed as 'woo hoos' and 'yahoos' filled the air. Proud parents wiped moist eyes and tearful teachers smiled congratulatory glances. Underclassmen waved their hands in the air as administrators absorbed the exultation of another successful ending to the school year.

In all the commotion, Mr. Sain navigated through the crowd, up the stairs to the stage, and to the podium. Composing himself, he raised his arms in the air and slowly lowered them to subdue the excitement. The noise subsided as Mr. Sain prepared to close the ceremony by giving Paul a double thumbs up.

"Thank you, Paul, and to the senior class for an inspiring evening. In fact, I would even like to add a quotation which I have run across in my readings and has mysteriously entered my thoughts. Although I am not sure of its accuracy, I do believe it was stated by Orrin Hatch who is an

American politician." Mr. Sain looked to the ceiling as he tried to find the correct wording that was dancing in his head. "It goes something like this. "There is a good reason they call these ceremonies 'commencement exercises.' Graduation is not the end, it is the beginning.'"

COMMUNICATION

That night, Paul lay awake in his bed replaying the evening's activities in his head. His thoughts wandered from when he first began worrying about deciding on the topic of his speech to its final delivery. He recalled the restless nights, the fleeting ideas, the potential unpreparedness and the anxiety he encumbered upon himself. He remembered burdening himself with thoughts of defeat and possibly being unable to finish the assignment.

But, just as quickly, his mind returned to Sunny View Park. He smiled as he recollected strolling across its grounds in the spring. He reviewed the admiration he had for the rebirth of nature and its return of wildlife. Visioning his statuesque comrade, 'The Professor' brought him comfort. He, too, identified with it, becoming a teacher. He thought of the friendship he forged with Timothy and the loyalty of Silas. Then, contentedly, he remembered the old man.

But, where was Barnaby now? Why had he never recently reappeared? Had something bad happened to him? Did anyone else know anything about him? Would he ever hear from him, again?

Becoming restless, Paul pushed down his covers and got out of bed. The eerie glow of the full moon supplied enough light to guide him to his window. He looked out into the cloudless nighttime sky and studied the constellations. Cassiopeia stared back at him. Moon shadows graced the yard. A calmness overcame him as he turned to go back to his bed.

But, as he passed his dresser, a glimmer caught his eye. A reflection of light where he normally laid his wallet captured his attention. Paul reached over and flicked on the light. There, next to his keys was a penny. It was no ordinary penny. It was a silver penny. Paul picked it up and examined it. The date on it was 1943. He then noticed a recipe sized note card upon which the penny had rested. As he picked up the paper and studied closely, Paul whispered to himself its inspiring words of wisdom . . . , "I will prepare and someday my chance will come' - Abraham Lincoln."

www.ingramcontent.com/pod-product-compliance
Lightning Source LLC
Chambersburg PA
CBHW071315200626
46813CB00015B/2209